A

Celia Dale's first nov~~el was published in 1943. She has since~~ written ten others, *Sheep's Clothing* (Penguin, 1989) being her most recent. This collection and her story, 'Lines of Communication', won the 1986 Crime Writers' Association Veuve Clicquot Short Story Award.

She has worked as a book reviewer and as a publisher's adviser. Many of her stories have been heard on radio and adapted for television. Celia Dale lives in Highgate, North London.

Celia Dale

A personal call
and other stories

PENGUIN BOOKS

PENGUIN BOOKS

Published by the Penguin Group
27 Wrights Lane, London w8 5tz, England
Viking Penguin Inc., 40 West 23rd Street, New York, New York 10010, USA
Penguin Books Australia Ltd, Ringwood, Victoria, Australia
Penguin Books Canada Ltd, 2801 John Street, Markham, Ontario, Canada l3r 1b4
Penguin Books (NZ) Ltd, 182–190 Wairau Road, Auckland 10, New Zealand

Penguin Books Ltd, Registered Offices: Harmondsworth, Middlesex, England

First published by Constable & Co. 1986
Published in Penguin Books 1990
1 3 5 7 9 10 8 6 4 2

Made and printed in Great Britain by
Richard Clay Ltd, Bungay, Suffolk
Filmset in Ehrhardt (Linotron 202)

For Michael Shaw

Contents

A personal call (*Winter's crimes* 1977)   9

Into the desert (*Cornhill Magazine* 1956)   18

Black museum (*Winter's crimes* 1980)   29

Something to take back (*Winter's tales* 1966)   42

Juno's swans (*Winter's crimes* 1972)   63

Madame Mantis (*Queen Magazine* 1939)   73

Lines of communication   79

The funny side (*Sphere Magazine* 1939)   86

Tenants (*Midnight ghost book* 1978)   95

Good investments (*Mystery Guild anthology* 1980)   106

What's to become of the pussies? (*Winter's crimes* 1969)   114

Moon daisy (*After midnight ghost book* 1980)   122

The better part of valour (*Winter's tales* 1975)   135

Business lunch (*John Creasey's crime collection* 1985)   152

A day like any other (*Sketch magazine* 1946)   159

A natural death (*Winter's tales* 1976)   164

Coming south (*Winter's crimes* 1973)   175

Old Tom (*Winter's tales* 1981)   181

*

A personal call

*

Every working day since his return from honeymoon Stanley
Drew left the canteen as soon as he had finished his lunch, put on
his raincoat, walked down the broad factory road to the wire gates,
turned left to the telephone kiosk in the alley beyond the bus stop,
and rang up his wife; personal calls were not allowed on company
lines.

'Hullo?' Her voice was very young.

'Is that you, dear? It's me. How are you?'

'Fine.'

'Had your dinner, have you?'

'In a sec.'

'What you having?'

'Oh – cheese, beans . . . I've not thought yet.'

'Have more than a snack, dear.'

'Yes, I will.'

'What you been doing?'

'I've made the kitchen curtains but I run out of rufflette. I'll pop
out later and get some.'

'Shall I bring you some home? I can get it easy.'

'No thanks, Stan, I want them up by this evening. They'll look
ever so pretty, all those frills.'

'You're a real little home-maker, pet.'

'Well . . .'

'You're a real little wife too, d'you know that?'

She giggled. 'I'd best get back to it, then.'

'Eat a proper dinner, now. And then you'll go to the shops?'

'That's right.'

'Okay, pet, then. Take care. I'm thinking of you.'

And indeed he was, even as the months grew into a year or more. For he could never lose the wonder, the nervous protective gratitude, that he, down his forties, not long released from an invalid mother, should have captured a girl as young and lovely as Cindy. Not much more than half his age, thick brown hair, eyes with lashes like a film star and a figure to match; he'd thought her perfect when he first set eyes on her, both of them part of a package tour to the Costa Brava, he alone, she with two other girls, laughing and showing off in their bikinis. Except that some mornings she didn't appear till nearly midday, looking washed out and sad – the food upset her, perhaps. She'd soon perk up, though; and when all three of them started to tease him flirtatiously, draw him out of himself, it was she that stayed with him when the others ran off. She lay on the sand beside him, her eyes closed, her hair fanned out on a towel, and surreptitiously he drank her in – arched ribs, breasts in their little cups, navel, round thighs where just a tendril of wiry hair escaped from her briefs. He had to turn over on to his stomach when he saw that, breathing deep, ashamed of his own pale flesh and the little paunch and his gnarled, old-looking feet.

Nevertheless, she seemed to like him. And the night before the holiday ended, made bold by plonk and group jollification, he took her outside under the hotel pine trees and kissed her. Her response drove him wild. He hardly saw the room she led him to, or heard her assurances that the girls she shared it with were well away downstairs in the bar, or had a coherent thought until he found himself back in his own room at past two o'clock in the morning, his room-mate solidly snoring.

He stayed close to her all the way back to London, carried her bags, cherished her. In the airport bus he asked her to marry him, and she said yes.

'Hullo?'

'Is that you, dear? It's me. Where are you? It rang ten times.'

'I was in the toilet.'

'Oh – sorry, dear. Not an upset?'

'Course not.'

'How've you been?'

'I'm giving the lounge a turn-out. All those old cycling magazines, d'you want them?'

'Well . . .'

'They're cluttering up. And I can't see you on a bike.' She giggled.

'Well, okay, dear. Throw them out.'

'Okay.'

'Had your dinner yet?'

'In a sec.'

'Have more than a snack, pet. An egg, milk . . .'

'I may do.'

'You've got to take care, sweetheart.'

Three months after their marriage she miscarried. The blood poured from her, more than he could believe possible at such an early stage, and he knew he would kill himself next day if they came to him in the hospital waiting-room and told him she was dead. They did not; she recovered, but wan and saying little. Beneath his anxiety, devotion and relief ran a tiny flame of pride that, at his age, he had been so potent. They had married within a month of meeting so it must have happened at once, perhaps even on that dizzying night in Spain. He would do it again, but not yet. It took her a long time to be her old self again – perhaps she never was, quite. More quiet, a little bit touchy, easily tired . . .

She was so young, they could afford to wait. Now he knew he could do it he was content to wait till she came around, and meanwhile cherish her, protect her, swaddle her in his loving pride.

'Hullo?'

'Is that you, dear? It's me. Where were you?'

'When?'

'Ten minutes ago. It rang and rang.'

'I was at the shops.'

'At dinner-time?'

'Yes.'

'You never go to the shops dinner-time.'

'I run out of milk.'

'Didn't he call?'

'He was late.'

'Well, I was worried.'

'What about?'

'You not answering.'

'For goodness' sake, Stan . . .'

'I like to know where you are, dear. I get anxious.'

'Don't be daft.'

'I know where you are from the number of times it rings. Six times it's the kitchen. Eight times it's the lounge. Ten times it's the bedroom or maybe the toilet.'

'And twenty times I've fallen downstairs running to answer it and broken my bloody neck.'

'Don't say that, pet. That's not funny.'

'Honestly, Stan . . . I can't spend my life on the end of the phone.'

'I like you to be there when I ring, though, sweetheart, otherwise I worry. You're always there dinner-time. I don't want you out when I ring, dear, it upsets me.'

She didn't reply.

'What have you been doing?' he asked placatingly.

'I told you. I went to the shops.'

'But at home? It's wash day, isn't it?'

'Yes. I think the machine's on the blink. I've not been able to do it all.'

'I'll have a look when I get home. You take it easy, dear.'

He was handy about the house, more house-proud than she was once the novelty of having her own home had worn off. She had altered the place completely, got rid of everything his mother had liked and he had grown up with; re-papered, re-painted, doing much of the work herself – perhaps that was why she

12

miscarried. At weekends he'd helped her, doting and proud of her energy and her small tight buttocks in the paint-stained jeans and her hair flopping into her eyes as she stretched for the ceiling, paint splashing over them both, for she was very slapdash. He went round after her, cleaning up; brought her tea when she lay exhausted, splayed out on the settee; cooked the supper. He couldn't afford a new three-piece suite but they'd chosen new stretch covers together; and the bedroom had been transformed into a lady's boudoir, all peach satin and nylon frills and fragrance from a dozen different bottles of lord knew what.

But all that was at first. Now things ran on an even keel, there was nothing much more to be done in the house except keep it clean and tidy. She hadn't a great deal to fill her time, which was why he liked to know where she was when he rang, to hear her voice and let her hear his, know he was thinking about her. And thinking about how a kid would fill her time, she should surely be ready for it now . . .

It rang six times.

'Hullo?'

'Is that you, dear? It's me. Where were you?'

'In the kitchen.'

'You're out of breath. What you been doing?'

'I slipped on the mat, answering the phone.'

'Did you hurt yourself, pet?'

'No, I'm okay. I just slipped.' Her breath was more normal now.

'Well, take care, dear. What you been doing?'

'Oh – ironing, odds and ends. You know.'

'Had your dinner yet?'

'Just going to. Beans on toast. The toast's on, Stan, I don't want it to burn.'

'Right, dear – you run off. Poach yourself an egg, pet, beans isn't enough.'

'Okay. Bye.'

13

'Take care, dear . . .'

A kid would fill her time, slow her down. Two years married, over eighteen months since the miscarriage. Time enough. High time.

'Was that him?'

'Who else.'

'Nip in.'

'Mmm . . .'

'Christ, your feet's freezing.'

'What d'you expect, running downstairs? Warm them.'

'Ouch!'

'I just made it, though. Six rings, and I'm in the kitchen.'

'You mean he counts them?'

'Every one. Ten and I'm in the bedroom. And what'd I be doing there at twelve-fifty-five p.m., I ask you?'

'I got the answer right here.'

It rang thirteen times. She was very out of breath.

'Where were you?'

'Down the garden.'

'It's pouring with rain.'

'A dog got in – a big black dog, like an Alsatian, it was digging up your dahlias. I run out to chase it off.'

'You be careful, dear. Alsatians can be savage.'

'I know. This one run off.'

'How've you been?'

'Ropey. Last night upset me, Stan.'

'I'm sorry, pet.'

'No, it upset me. I don't want to talk about it.'

'Cindy . . .'

'I've got a headache, Stan. I'm going to lie down.'

'You do that, sweetheart, take an aspirin. Shall I bring some home? Take care, now . . .' But she had hung up.

He bought a dozen pink carnations from the man by the Tube station and took them home to her. She still had a headache.

'Him?'

'Yes.'

'Cuddle up. You're freezing.'

'He's driving me nuts. He suffocates me. He's like some great suffocating smothering blanket. Every day the same thing. Morning – bye-bye, dear, see you later, take care. Dinner-time – is that you, dear, it's me, how've you been? Evening – It's me, dear, I'm back, had a good day? And later on – are you sleepy, dear, how's your head? It's not my bloody head he's on about. He's driving me nuts!'

'Ssh, chickykins, ssh . . .'

'Oh, Dave, if only you hadn't run out on me!'

'I couldn't help it, could I? I mean, I had to go where the money was, didn't I? I didn't know you was in the club, did I?'

'Would you have stayed if you had, Dave?'

'I dunno. Straight, I dunno. But now I would. Now I'd stay with you for ever. Cindy, d'you believe me?'

'I don't know.'

'You gotta believe me. I'm nuts about you, Cindy . . .'

She answered at once. 'Stan?'

'Hullo, dear. It's me.'

'Stan, have you had my pills?'

'Pills?'

'Pills, pills. The pills I take very morning. The pills so I won't get pregnant. Those pills!'

'I put them down the toilet, dear.'

'You . . . !' It was almost a scream.

'You don't need them, pet. Not any more. They're not good for you to go on taking regular, it's not natural.'

He could sense her struggling for control, envisage her standing in their narrow hall, the receiver clenched in her hand.

'I put them down the toilet,' he repeated gently.

After a moment she said, 'You know I'll get some more, don't you. I'll go to the doctor and get some more.'

'I'd rather you didn't, dear. Anyway, the surgery's not till this evening and the shops'll be shut by then. You'll have to give it a miss for a day or two.'

She hung up. He wondered if, after all, he had done the right thing. Walking back to the factory, he decided he had.

'Dave, Dave, supposing I am?'

'You've got some now, haven't you?'

'But there was two days without. I was two days without!'

'It'd be mine, wouldn't it?'

'Oh, Dave – d'you think I'd let it be his? I can't bear him to touch me, I can't stand his great hands and his soppy great eyes and his face and his voice and his . . .'

The telephone rang.

'Don't answer it.'

'I must.'

'Why? Let him sweat.'

'I have to. Else he keeps on and on . . .'

'Cindy . . .'

She ran out of the room, naked, her face wet with tears.

It was a bad November, dank and sullen, dark by tea-time, often dark midday with rain sheeting down from heavy clouds. He finished his lunch in the canteen, put on his raincoat, took his umbrella and went out, down the broad factory road to the wire gates, turned left to the telephone kiosk he had used each working day since his honeymoon, in the alley beyond the bus stop.

The bell rang six times.

'Is that you, dear? It's me.'

'Yes.'

'Were you in the kitchen?'

'Yes.'

'How've you been?'

'Okay.'

'Had your dinner yet?'

'Soon.'

'Don't just have a snack. Have something nourishing, dear, an egg . . .'

The door of the kiosk opened behind him and a heavy, lorry-driver's spanner crashed down on his head. He staggered, sagged, put up an arm. A cloth of some kind went over his head and the spanner crashed down again, and again, and once more. His knees gave, he folded slowly below the vandal-proof shelves, moved feebly, groaned, died.

A hand in a rubber glove dropped the spanner beside him, then, after a moment, took up the receiver that spun on its plastic cord.

'Is that you? It's me.' The voice was out of breath, taking great gulps of air.

She too was breathless. 'Have you . . . ?'

'Yes. I'll ring you. Don't go out.'

'No.'

'Stay by the phone. Okay?'

'Take care.'

The door opened and shut quickly. The huddled shape with its muffled head was no more than a darker shadow on the floor of the kiosk as the rain beat heavily from the dark sky. The receiver had been replaced.

*

Into the desert

*

Jerry was hoping I wouldn't make a scene. He stood, not looking
at me, with the half-smile he always used for official interviews
and Press conferences, and his eyes screwed up against the glare.
The runway had little bubbles in it from the heat, and the sandy
ground stretching on either side seemed to shift like a bog under
the haze. Even in the shade of the airport office (if you could call it
that) the air was tepid.

'Here it comes,' I said, my voice quite steady. The 'plane was
taxi-ing cautiously towards us, small and angular like an elderly
locust, and a swarm of noisy, brown-faced men ran at its tail and
under its wings, helping it.

'The Space Ship'. He had a habit of putting things in capital
letters that somehow, for me, always made them funny. If you
were funny in the Compound, where even the water tasted of oil,
the other families thought you were getting at them. You had to be
very careful, living in a closed community like that. You had to be
like everyone else. Roger was, and I always had been, until I met
Jerry. If I thought about it, all the times I had spent with him, right
back to the first meeting at the oil company's reception when
Roger took over the Public Relations job, seemed glinted over
with laughter, with wonder and warmth at seeing things new
through Jerry's half-cynical, half-tender eyes.

'The flowers are lovely.' They were fainting already, their scent
strengthening into rankness. 'I wish things would grow at El
Hait.'

'You must get down to it and build the Garden Beautiful,' he
said. 'I wonder where your luggage is?'

'There.' The men were running in and out from the shed to the

18

'plane now, their gowns flapping around the suitcases they held under their arms and in their hands. They never stopped calling to each other, and now the engine had started up, roaring and coughing.

He touched my elbow. 'You'd better get in.'

'Not yet.' I was not going to make a scene, I was not even going to cry, but I spoke too urgently. He looked away over my head to the yellow hills in the distance. 'Will you come to El Hait soon, Jerry, d'you think?' Anyone might ask him that, it was ordinary small talk.

'I wouldn't know. They talk of sending me to Greece.'

'Journalists lead such interesting lives,' I said, and laughed; but it wasn't really very funny. 'You will write to me, Jerry? Your letters are such fun to get.'

'My Public.'

'Mine are dull, I know. There's nothing amusing to tell you about, ever. But you know what they try to say, don't you?'

'Dear Jennifer,' he said, very gently, and I felt the tears coming, I couldn't help it.

'Jerry . . .' I said, and clutched his arm. It was hairy and warm and had a scar on the underside from a shell splinter when he was a War Correspondent. 'Jerry, please . . .'

Somewhere inside the airport someone screamed, there was an outburst of shouting, men mostly but with a woman's overriding them all, shrill and inexhaustible, in Arabic but with French and Spanish mixed in. We turned to look as the door was pushed open and a woman thrust through, struggling in the grip of two nervous policemen. She turned, swinging a snakeskin handbag to strike off the helmet of one while kicking the other under the knee. They both let go, sweating, and she shook herself into place.

'Camels!' she said, and smoothed back her hair, staring at Jerry and me arrogantly out of eyes lined round with mascara. 'And my luggage – have you stolen that, you sons of filth?'

'It is there, on the 'plane, going on now and you after it!' panted one of the policemen, his face thin with spite. Behind them in the doorway a crowd was peering, talking loudly.

'Then why am I kept waiting?' asked the woman. 'And if so much as a lock is undone I shall complain to my friend.'

She stepped out into the sunlight on heels so thin that they sank into the tarmac, and approached the 'plane. The ladder was high, and it was difficult for her to mount it in so tight a skirt. The porters sighed voluptuously as she disappeared inside.

'You'd better go,' said Jerry. 'You've certainly got a colourful fellow-passenger.'

The sun thundered down on us as we crossed to the 'plane.

'Jerry . . . If I can't stand it there any more . . .' I could hear my voice but I couldn't control it. It was like being under an anaesthetic, or very very drunk. 'If I tell him, if I really have to tell him and come back here to you . . .'

His hand was firm on my elbow, easing me up the steps. 'I shan't be here, most likely, most of the time. I'll be moving about.'

'Where will be you be?' The 'plane was vibrating under my feet, and the porters pushed between us, taking away the ladder. I clutched at the lintels of the door, staring down at him, but he swam in my tears.

'I'll write to you,' he said, and stepped back. The porters pushed me inside, slamming the door. Almost at once we began to move, and I staggered as the little 'plane bumped for the take-off. There were no stewards on this ramshackle service between the capital and the Emirate, and I was the only passenger except for the woman.

We rose and circled and did not crash, and I did not care. I knew the dun wastes of the airfield, the sheds and the road leading back to the town, the houses like sugar-cubes emptied into a fold of the hills. I knew it from a dozen trips, a dozen holidays. The Compound people called them 'leaves', as though we were soldiers and the holidays necessary medicine to be taken regularly; but to me they were shining, extravagant, to be saved for and squandered and saved for again, not in money but in – what? Love? Richness? Experience? All those, everything, there's no single word to encompass them all. The Compound people said: 'Going on leave? Pity Roger can't go with you,' and I always

20

agreed, my smile most ordinary; but whether they noticed my eyes or my voice or the lightness of my walk I don't know and had never cared.

I could cry now, huddled in the hard little seat.

A cloud like incense came to me, and a thin hand, brown, not very clean, with long chipped crimson nails and heavy rings, offered a cigarette-case. She said in French: 'They calm the nerves.'

She was right, and I took one. She lit it from a gold-seeming lighter, the bangles clashing back from her wrist. 'You're nervous at flying? I, never. I am fatalist.' She sat down in the seat opposite, the narrow skirt riding up to her knees. She had thin hairy legs, and wore snakeskin sandals that showed red-lacquered, ugly toes. 'They say that smoking discolours the teeth, but I have never found it so.' She smiled, and her teeth were large and white, save for two that were gold. 'Now. Relax yourself. There's no more to be done till we reach El Hait.'

She sat back, inhaling and letting the smoke plume slowly from her nostrils. She was small and thin, save for two sudden inflexible ripenesses that filled the bosom of her jacket. The jacket and its skirt were of some moiré sort of stuff that looked like snakeskin, grey and mottled, with too-square shoulders and one sleeve pulling a little at the seams, and the whole thing creased as though it had been slept in. Her limbs were brown and wiry, and her face also beneath its heavy make-up. She wore powder too light for her powerful nose, her mouth crimson, eyes brilliant. A mass of dry black hair with a henna streak in it hung down over her shoulders.

'You visit El Hait?' she asked after a moment.

'I live there.'

'Ah, you've been taking a holiday. That's good. Me, I never take holidays. All life for me is work and play both. You see, I am an artiste. Perhaps you have seen me dance?'

'I'm afraid . . .'

'Algiers, Cairo, Tel Aviv, Tunis, everywhere – Elvira the Serpent. My act is very celebrated. I am specialist in the dance of the snakes, very lifelike, very artistic. I writhe and twist the arms so, also the belly, also the head, all, in fact. I have danced for Farouk.'

'Really?'

'I have much public, many important friends.'

'You're going to dance at El Hait?'

Her eyes grew wary, and she threw back her hair haughtily. 'Who can tell? It is for fate.'

We were silent, finishing our cigarettes, the 'plane shaking and roaring, and all around the luminous, ever-lasting sky. Once the curtain over the pilot's cabin was drawn aside and a brown face stared at us for a moment. The woman dropped her cigarette on the floor and ground it out with her heel, then turned and began to rummage among her suitcases. They too were of snakeskin, save where the covering was torn and showed the fibre underneath, and one had a handle tied together with rope. She found a basket and from it took a bottle and some oranges.

'Whiskey?' I shook my head. 'You'll excuse me?' She uncorked the bottle and tilted it to her mouth, the brown throat stretched and gulping. 'It helps the nerves,' she said, recorking it. 'I have had much to endure just lately. For an artiste life is never too easy. One has friends, but one has also enemies. Camels!' She made a gesture entirely Gallic.

'There seemed some trouble at the airport . . . ?'

'Pah!' If my friend had been in power they would never have dared! As it was, I would never had stayed anyway, not if they had crawled to me. They do not deserve art.'

'You were appearing there?'

'I had intended. I came there from Bizerta. Before that, Tangier.'

'You travel a great deal.'

'It is the artiste's life. I know much of the world. I have appeared even in Marseilles, they had my picture big outside the cabaret. That was before that old fool Pétain, naturally. All my life has been as a dancer, since I was four years old. My mother taught me to move the arms and the head, she was from the South where

22

the movements are very fine, and always I practised, worked and practised, it was my métier, you understand? That is why I say work and play for me are the same thing. When I was thirteen only I had an engagement in Casablanca, you know Casablanca? Well, I was in Casablanca, Oran, Rabat, Tripoli, all over.' Her face became suddenly savage. 'And of all dungheaps in the world, that we have just left stinks the worst!'

'It's better than El Hait.'

'For you perhaps. It has for you no doubt a certain attraction, hein?' She showed the white and gold teeth in a smile, and her eyes appraised me as a farmer might appraise a sow for breeding purposes, with a look not unsympathetic but strictly practical. 'He's a nice boy, that one. American?'

'No.'

'Americans are best. In Oran I had many American friends after the landings. I was at Lindy's Dive, you know it perhaps, near the harbour? They used to shout and whistle when I appeared, and sometimes they would try and join in and we would give a very interesting dance, difficult, of course, because often they were very drunk, but I had much success. There are no Americans now. And Cairo since Nasser . . . !' She made the gesture again. 'There are not many places an artiste cares to go back to. The dungheap we have just left is as bad as the rest . . .'

'What was the trouble?'

'Trouble? There was no trouble.' She shook back her hair fiercely. 'They think they throw me out but I had gone already, my ticket was taken, I can prove that, all I needed was the money. I would not stay in that cesspool. If my friend there had not been in difficulties just now it would have been a different story, believe me. They made talk about papers, but my papers are as good as any, I can go where I like, I have many official stamps, look, you look at my papers.'

She burrowed into the snakeskin handbag, amongst a debris of ragged handkerchiefs, a stocking or two, lipstick stubs and greasy powder-puffs, cigarettes, creased letters, and produced her passport. It was the green folder of the stateless, shabby and worn.

She held it open with one long dirty nail, sitting sideways on the edge of the seat so that I could see it. 'You see? It's good, isn't it? See, many stamps and all in order.' She kept her thumb over the date of birth, but the photograph stared up at us haggardly. 'It's not a good likeness, of course, it doesn't do me justice. I had been ill, there had been much trouble – my God, I don't like to remember it!' She snapped the passport shut. 'For my friends I have special postcards of myself in costume. The cabarets sell them, you know, and many people buy them, they are very artistic and could be shown anywhere. Unfortunately I have none with me just now, those sons of camels at the police station took them last night.' She spat suddenly into the aisle, then yawned and lay back in the seat. 'Ah well, all is with fate. There must be other places in the world, after all.'

She shut her eyes and almost at once was asleep. I looked out at the empty sky and our shadow crawling over the empty wastes below, the stones and the scrub and the horny bushes and the huddling green round a well. El Hait was little more than all that, except that there were concrete roads and wire fences and the houses were not made of mud and dung but of prefab units flown out by the Company and erected at well-planned intervals. Trees grew in the Compound too, only certain kinds and not very many, but still trees; and the high-ups, the executives with the biggest salaries, had grass, sprayed everlastingly by the garden boys so long as there was no drought. There was a cinema and two club houses, one for the high-ups and one for the rest. Roger and I belonged to the first, of course, and we had a tree inside our wire fence; but not grass.

I clenched my fists on my knees and stared down at the rocks and the scrub, and I thought: It's no good, it's all over, you know that, don't be a fool. Leave it now as it is, don't cling and importune and beg. He was nice to you, wasn't he, there was no quarrel. Maybe you've imagined the whole thing, and he's sitting down now, in the shaded room with the rugs and the old typewriter and the lilies you put in a vase only this morning, and beginning a wonderful letter, a letter to Roger even, perhaps, telling him, explaining the way it happened, saying we have to be together ... Don't be a fool, I thought, watching the blind crawling shadow, it's over. You'll never go back to that room and that glory again. You'll never go anywhere now but back to Roger. That is, if he hasn't found out.

When I opened my eyes it was dusk in the 'plane, and the sky the tenderest pinky-green. She was awake opposite, staring out of the window, smoking. In the twilight the hollows of her eyes and cheeks were deep.

She said abruptly: 'We're nearly there, hein?'

'Yes, I think so.' I began to tidy myself, noting with weariness in my mirror that my eyes were now hardly red at all.

'What are they like there?'

'Who?'

'The officials.'

'At the airfield? I hardly know. They all know me, you see, they know all of us from the Compound.'

'Perhaps there's one just a little more sympathetic than the others? Artistic, perhaps, one who admires beautiful things?'

I considered. 'I really don't know. It's never come up.'

She gave me a hard glance, like an animal staring into a room from the darkness. 'No, of course for you it would not come up. It's your home here. Well, all is with fate.'

She crushed out the cigarette and sat up, running the long fingers through her hair with a rattle of jewellery. She opened her handbag and began to re-do her face, the powder clouding us both. Eyebrows, eyelashes, teeth, hair, throat, all were examined fiercely, squinting into the small lid of her compact.

The curtain at the pilot's cabin was pushed back and the pilot appeared. 'Ah, ladies, you're ready? We shall be there in three minutes.'

She flashed him a smile of utter confidence. 'Yes, my friend, we're ready.'

The lights of the airfield were on, pathetically sparse in the now almost darkness, strung out like nightlights round the lamp of the office sheds. The noise of the engine changed, and we could feel this tin cigar in which we were confined shudder against the altering air.

Her hands were clenched on the snakeskin bag. 'Madame,' she said harshly, 'will you speak for me?'

I looked across at her in surprise. 'But of course. That is, if it's necessary. Although I don't know there's much I can say . . . ?'

'It is sometimes of great value to have someone to speak for one. To show one is not without friends. It weighs much with officials. If you would say you have seen me dance, or have heard well of me. Perhaps even your husband might speak for me . . .'

I said quickly: 'Of course I'll do what I can.' Not Roger – dear me no, not Roger! It would really be best if Roger didn't see her at all, he was always so anxious about the morals of our natives and of the young bachelors come out from England.

There was a bump and a jar, a frenzy from the engine, then silence. From outside the voices of porters sounded, the thud of the ladder and scrabbling at the door. We stood up and gathered our baggage. She bobbed her head to stare out at the lighted airshed, and I saw that she was trembling.

Roger stood under the lamp, square, well-groomed, rather handsome. I smiled and hurried towards him. He took my bag and asked did I have a good journey, and in the tone of his voice, the cold folds of his smile, I knew. Someone had told him.

I talked on quickly, smiling and being very gay, and he followed me into the shed and saw to the rest of my luggage and spoke to the passport man, whom of course I knew well. He was the rather handsome one, his exquisite khaki uniform hardly a darker shade than his skin. He was very polite and hoped I'd had a good leave, and signalled my baggage out to the car without even glancing at it.

'Well,' I said brightly to Roger, 'shall we go?'

As I turned I heard the clatter of heels behind me. The door was pushed open and she came in, clutching her snakeskin handbag and the basket with the bottle of whiskey in it. She was smiling, her head high, and the bracelets jangled as she moved. An official came behind her, not smiling, and said something to the handsome one. She broke in, her smile unchanging and her eyes flickering from one to the other. They looked at her passport and at her, and their faces became stony.

'Oh, Captain,' I said, 'If you can deal swiftly with this lady, my husband and I can give her a lift into the town.'

The handsome one turned. 'Please do not disturb yourself, madame. There are a few formalities to be gone into.'

'We're in no hurry,' I said, 'We'll wait. I'm sure you won't keep her long.'

I could feel Roger's anger and embarrassment swelling at my back, and I saw her look from me to him with practised hope that froze into impassivity.

The handsome one smiled, flapping her passport absently on the desk. 'I fear it will take a little time, madame. There are always tedious formalities to be gone into when one comes to the end of a journey. I'm sure this lady would not wish you to wait.'

I looked at her. She held her head well, the dry black hair massed on the thin shoulders and the eyes very bright between the mascara. She showed the two gold teeth.

'Please do not wait.' She said clearly, 'These little men must always make themselves important. You will come to see me dance in a few days, I hope, and bring your friends.'

I followed Roger out to the car. It was quite dark now, and I could not see his expression at all. 'Who the hell was that?' he said.

'She's a dancer. She talked to me on the journey. They wouldn't have her in Faqualla, they put her on the 'plane.'

'They won't have her here either, if I know the signs,' he said, and got into the car.

'But where can she go? She must go somewhere?'

'Not if nobody will have her.' He started the engine, but sat for a moment with hands on the wheel. In the faint light from the dashboard I could see them, and the shadow of his white jacket. He nearly said something, and I sat breathless with fear, breathless with panic, the panic of an animal that finds the burrow finally closed to it. Then he let in the clutch and turned the car out on to the road.

As we went past I turned my head and looked into the airshed. Through the windows I could see the officials, joined by a third now, poring over the documents they had laid out on the desk. In the opposite doorway the porters jostled, giggling behind thin hands. The woman sat on her snakeskin baggage, very neat and still, the tight skirt showing the knees, the improbable breasts rigid in the creased silk. She was smoking, blowing the smoke from her high nostrils, her head arrogant. Her face was impassive, her eyes looked at nothing at all.

Black museum

*

I have never disliked anyone as much as I came to dislike Reggie Tyrrell. I admit he had magnetism – the magnetism that comes not only from immense conceit but from the cleverness that justifies it, to some extent. Certainly he had no physical charms to be conceited about – although he was. He was a short, wiry man – stringy, really, because when I met him first he was in his forties and the muscle that had made him (so he all too often told one) a fine athlete at university had shrunk to sinew. In bathing trunks and burned by the sun (he lived half the year in a villa in southern Spain, up in the hills behind Marbella) he looked like a bundle of leather bootlaces or one of the small, slightly sinister lizards that darted about his terraces, gulping flies.

One of the flies he gulped was my friend Pamela, which is how I met him. She and her mother went for a spring holiday in Marbella and when they came back Pamela had a sort of muted glow about her. Pamela is a muted kind of person. We met at school, where she was a prefect but never Head Girl. Then she was secretary to some big wheel in a faceless conglomerate and for years had an affair with one of the directors – a nice man, I often met him, but of course heavily married and no intention of getting free. And then he died of a coronary one day at home and the first Pamela heard of it was when she came into the office next morning. She had to hide it all and sweat it out alone – I saw a lot of her then and I hope I helped. But it broke her up and she became even more muted than she'd been before, allowing herself to be dominated by her tiresome mother.

My marriage was on the rocks soon after – no special reason, I just couldn't stand him any more, he was so totally boring – so I didn't see much of her for a while; but we always kept in touch, and when we met soon after her holiday she had, as I said, this sort of muted glow.

'Did you meet anybody?' I asked. I always asked that.

'Well ...' She has this fair skin that actually blushes sometimes, a nuisance but rather sweet. 'We met Reggie Tyrrell.'

'Who?'

'Reginald Tyrrell. You know, the writer.'

'What, the crime man? That Tyrrell?'

'Yes. He said he'd ring up when he came back to England but I don't expect he will.'

I must admit I was impressed. Everyone knew Reginald Tyrrell, if not from his books then from his journalism, radio and television. He'd made himself the absolute ultimate expert in murder; apart from his apparently inexhaustible flow of books and articles on crime, not a symposium or a TV discussion or a preface to some book about murder but Reginald Tyrrell's name appeared on it. He had enormous knowledge, not only of well-known cases but of the more obscure; and he was a past-master at squeezing the last drop of blood from a corpse – no matter how well investigated already, he'd find some new thing about it, or some new psychological slant. And somehow he always managed to make it sexy; an old lady poisoned for her money in 1892 somehow had undertones of unspeakable sexual nastiness when Reggie wrote about it.

'What's he like?' I asked.

'He's rather sweet.'

Sweet! I ask you!

He did ring her up when he came back to London in May, and by August they were married. He'd been married three times before and was very vain of the fact. I think Pamela deliberately kept me from meeting him until it was practically all sealed and signed – I suppose she knew I wouldn't approve. So I met him first at their

engagement party – Claridge's, no less, and nothing but champagne, and Pamela in a sort of daze but with a confidence I'd
never seen in her before. Masses of people there – minor Jet
Set and publishers and film and television people and other
authors whose names one knew and several high ranking
policemen and a famous pathologist. It was a really glossy
affair.

They were both by the door, receiving. 'So this is Dinah,' he
said, keeping my hand. 'Pam's best friend.'

I don't know what I'd expected. One knew his face, of course,
from photographs, but I hadn't realised he was so short and so
ugly. He was, as I've said, leathery, and only about five foot six.
His hair was greying but thick, rather wiry, worn rather too
long for a man over thirty; his nose was aggressive, his mouth
too broad. He had very big teeth. His eyes were grey, and he
used them to peer ardently at me as he still kept my hand, selling
me the idea of how good a friend I was to his bride-to-be
while at the same time a desirable woman. It was corny as
hell.

Later I saw him caressing the buttocks of some nubile young
columnist, kissing the hand of a television actress and the cheek
of a fashionable public relations lady. Not the way a man
should behave at his own engagement party. I avoided saying
goodbye to either of them and went home in a rage. Poor silly
Pamela!

I had to be friends with them both, of course – I even went to the
wedding – for I didn't want to drop Pamela after all these years
and I was sure she'd be needing a friend before long, married to
that self-satisfied shit. But, wonder of wonders, the marriage
seemed a success. When we dined together from time to time he
was almost cloyingly attentive to her while still managing to beam
a wolf gleam or two towards me from those slightly bloodshot
eyes. He was an amusing talker, but sooner or later always
brought the conversation round to his own subject – himself and

31

his mastery of criminology. Apart from his theories on the identity of Jack the Ripper or the murderer of Julia Wallace, he loved to embark on details of lesser known and usually squalid mysteries – poor middleaged prostitutes disembowelled on rubbish tips or drunken farmers poisoned by their moronic wives. More than this, he had a large collection of relics of various crimes of which he was disgustingly proud, acquired God knows how – from lawyers, detectives, pathologists, amongst whom he had a great number of acquaintances. It was his delight to take one on a tour round this beastly little Black Museum after dinner, when he would explain the relevance of that fragment of bloodstained wallpaper or the singular significance of the yellowed upper denture retrieved from some murderer's cabbage-patch. It was absolutely revolting.

But of course it was fascinating too. And he knew it – and knew how to exploit that fascination, the urge to life that fear of death promotes, the bizarre beneath the humdrum, the ultimate orgasm of violent death (his phrases, needless to say). After all, everyone likes a good murder; and Reggie's murders were very good, as his pretty house in St John's Wood, his villa in Spain, his three ex-wives, his Bentley and champagne and custom-made shirts proved.

They went off to the villa for the winter, and as I was rather preoccupied then with a new man (he didn't work out) I lost touch with them for a while. Pamela wrote and seemed happy. Then one day Reggie rang up. He was back in London ahead of Pamela to do a rush television adaptation of a famous trial, and he asked me to do some work for him – checking dates, researching death certificates – as he was short of time and hadn't a secretary. I was at a loose end just then, so I did. And when Pamela came back to London in April I went on working for him – it quite suited me not to be tied to a regular job. And I have to admit, it was rather fascinating.

Pamela looked blooming but she was more reserved. She had

always been quiet but whereas before it had been because she was uncertain and timid, now it held confidence. When we met for a girls' lunch and gossip she was very much Mrs Reginald Tyrrell; she wouldn't open up at all about him, not what he was actually *like*. All she would say was that he was 'very sweet', very generous; he worked very hard, they had lots of social life, they were very happy.

'Don't you find all those corpses and blood a bit much?' I asked, a bit bitchily, for her grande-damerie was beginning to irritate me. She was only Pamela, for God's sake!

She looked away for a moment, then back with a placid smile. 'I don't notice it. It's his work, after all.'

'But the Black Museum? Those bloodstained bits and pieces and all those ghastly photographs? Knowing he's back to dinner all freshly scrubbed from a sneak view of a post-mortem?'

She blushed. 'Don't be silly, Dinah.'

Of course what I really wanted to know was what he was like in bed. But I hadn't quite got the nerve to ask her that.

I went out to Rojas and stayed with them twice the next winter. I'd done some more research for him and took the results with me. He was easy to work for, very well organised, writing for three hours every morning and another two after tea, when we'd collate my material. The villa was beautiful, up in the hills with a distant view of the sea, with a swimming pool and a garden dripping with bougainvillea and geraniums in huge pots and a guest wing with its own terrace and little kitchen. They had a fair circle of friends out there, for Reggie was quite a celebrity, especially in an expatriate community. While he basked in it all, stroking the women and rattling off anecdotes of arsenic and old lace, Pamela ran the household quietly, speaking a careful Spanish to the plump, large-eyed local girls who cooked and cleared, an efficient wife and hostess. It was a pretty good life for my little school chum who had never managed to make it either to Head Girl or to Chairman's wife.

There was a big murder trial at the Old Bailey the following March (three Old Age Pensioners dug up in the garden of a Sunset Home and all for the sake of their pension books) and Reggie came back to London on his own for it, as he always did. Murder trials were for him what performances at La Scala or Covent Garden are to opera buffs – essential in themselves but also for being seen to be there. This time he wanted me not only to sit in on the trial with him as I had before but also to take notes of some disgusting details he ferretted out unofficially for the books he was planning to write, but that I refused. Going to trials, checking dates and death certificates and bequests in wills was one thing, formaldehyde and your actual murder scenes quite another, it turned me up and I wouldn't do it. So he borrowed a typist from the defence lawyer's office and used her – and that is just what I mean.

I couldn't believe it, not at first. I mean, it was so blatant. Even after Pamela came back for the summer, Tracy was still everywhere with him, all bangles and bubble-cut, typing away in the study in St John's Wood, trotting about after him to police stations and mortuaries and the houses of the bereaved with her notebook and biro at the ready. He had been used to typing direct himself, but now he spent hours shut up with Tracy dictating his material to her – or so it was assumed. She did go back to her own home at night, but often he drove her. I simply couldn't believe it.

Pamela gave no sign she noticed anything. She ran the house, hostessed his parties, stood as his lady everywhere, as quiet and undemanding as she had always been. She must have known – even she couldn't have been such a fool. Sometimes I caught a rather frosty glint in her eyes as she smiled at Tracy over their working lunch, but otherwise she gave absolutely no sign.

When she and Reggie went back to the villa in October, Tracy returned to her lawyers' office; the affair was apparently over.

'How do you manage without your faithful slave?' I asked maliciously when I stayed with them there before Christmas.

He gave me one of his lizard looks. 'Who d'you mean – Tracy?'

I nodded, he shrugged with a yellow-toothed grin. 'Perfectly well. I'm self-sufficient, you know.'

'Pamela must miss having her underfoot.'

'Me?' Pamela smiled coolly. 'It makes no difference to me. I really didn't notice her.'

Because of Tracy I began to keep a closer eye on Reggie, both on his solo returns to London as well as when I stayed with them at Rojas. In London I hadn't much chance; he came back for only a few days to attend yet another murder trial and this time he didn't suggest I went with him. Apart from dinner one evening, after which he insisted on showing me a new series of pictures of grisly forensic processes which, with great glee, he had managed to acquire from one of his slightly bent police contacts, he went his own way and was soon back at the villa. I think he realised that I now really mistrusted him, and although this seemed to amuse him and feed his vanity, he dropped me.

But I still did research for him – I could suit myself when I did it and the work itself had come to have a kind of fascination. I took the results out to him at Rojas on my first visit that winter and saw, with rising anger and dismay, that he was in pursuit of a monolithic Swedish girl, wife of one of the large foreign colony there, a blonde Valkyrie always half naked and a good head taller than he was. Again, Pamela seemed to notice nothing and treated Ingrid or whatever her name was with the same mild friendliness as everyone else at the vacuous social gatherings that made up life there. How she could have so little pride . . . !

When I went back the second time, in March, Ingrid and her husband had gone. The expatriate colony had shrunk a little, life was rather dull and Reggie was working. He had his own rooms at the end of the villa – bedroom, bathroom and study – and often wouldn't appear till drinks time at sundown. During the day Pamela and I lazed, swam in the pool, drove into the hills or along to Malaga. We didn't talk much; she had always been quiet and now the quiet had become a sort of withdrawal, at least from me –

she simply did not seem to want to talk about anything much. And I couldn't really bring myself to say anything to her that touched on Reggie.

The weather was wonderful – mild and blue and the grass on the hillsides still green and thick with tiny orchids. Down on the coast the package tourists had hardly yet begun and we could still shop and drink peacefully in the small core of what had once been a fishing village, now surrounded and submerged by concrete blocks of hotels, discos, supermarkets and souvenir shops. The black-clad housewives as yet still did their shopping in dark, almost hidden stores, the men as yet still sat gossiping in the bare-floored bars concealed by clicking bead curtains. The heart of the village as yet could still be heard beating before the summer blare of muzak drowned it out.

It was peaceful – a sort of stagnation really, I suppose. It soothed me, yet I was restless. I knew I ought to get back to London, find a real job to do instead of hanging round till Reggie wanted something. Yet I couldn't bring myself to leave; it was so beautiful; Pamela was my oldest friend.

I woke early one morning, just after dawn. The sky was like pearl, and I went out on to the terrace that ran the length of the house from the guest wing where I was, past the living quarters and on to Reggie's suite at the far end. Pamela's rooms were on the other side, the terrace ran right round. The air smelled of dew and grass and lemons and there wasn't a sound – until someone came in slippers out of Reggie's rooms at the far end and slapped quietly down the terrace steps to the garden below and out of sight. In the pale dawn light I could see quite well it was Paquita, the newish maid that made such wonderful paellas. And Reggie, wearing nothing but a towel slung over his boney shoulders, stood on the terrace and blew a kiss to her as she flitted away.

Thank God he was working and didn't appear all day. I don't know what I'd have done if I'd seen him earlier. Shock and fury possessed me. How could he! Tracy and Ingrid had been bad enough, blatant enough – but Paquita, a servant in his own house, and having her only a room or two away from his own wife! A maid, a servant who stank of sweat and garlic, who no doubt boasted and sniggered about him with the other servants, whose knowing eyes would also hold contempt. How could he – how *could* he! How could Pamela bear this humiliation? She had shut her eyes to all the others, for her own reasons, but could she shut her eyes to this? A servant, in her own house?

I got through the day somehow and the evening, watching them both like a cat. Pamela looked pale and strained, pleaded a headache; Reggie was jaunty as usual, a cravat knotted at his stringy throat, his gaze as bold as ever, brazen, his big teeth grinning. 'Ruth Ellis,' he said, 'that's who I'll do next. It's got everything – sex, jealousy, drink, the death penalty. You might turn up the cuttings, Dinah, when you go back – I know it all, of course, I was at the trial, and I've got photocopies of all the evidence. I shall get right inside the woman and her bunch of sleazy lovers, show what made them tick. The pub where she shot him's still there, of course, I knew it well at the time . . .' He went on like this and we listened. Then we went to bed.

Sex, jealousy, drink perhaps – they all lay smashed at the foot of the terrace next morning when the gardener raised the alarm. Reggie was wearing pyjamas this time, and he was dead.

The Spanish police are different from ours – very suave, very courteous, almost military in style. They waited until Pamela felt able to speak to them later that morning, when the tears had stopped, the sedative begun to work, and she was dressed, pale but calm. I sat beside her but she would not hold my hand, her fingers clenched and moving over a handkerchief. The officer explained to us what had happened: Señor Tyrrell had apparently been standing by the parapet of the terrace outside his bedroom at approximately 2 a.m. (according to the police doctor). He had a glass of whiskey in his hand (the fragments were shattered round his body) and had consumed a fair amount during the preceding hours. He had also perhaps consumed one or two of the sleeping pills found at his bedside ... 'Did Señor Tyrrell take sleeping pills, señora?'

Pamela nodded. 'Sometimes – when he was on a book. He found it hard to unwind.'

'So. He is drinking quite heavily during the evening, he takes the pills, goes out on to the terrace because perhaps still insomniac, takes perhaps another pill, takes certainly some more whiskey. He stands by the parapet, he becomes dizzy from the alcohol and the drug, he falls. In falling, I fear to say, he takes with him one of the heavy pots of geraniums that stand along the terrace, and it is that, crashing upon him, which – forgive me, señora – causes your husband's death. The fall alone, possibly not – many injuries, yes, but perhaps not fatal. The geranium pot, so full, so massive – by the will of God, yes.'

She began to cry. He regarded her with soft, lively black eyes. 'I will leave you now. There will be some formalities but nothing that need distress you too much, I think. My sincere condolences, señora – he was a distinguished member of our welcome foreign community.' He got to his feet, then paused. 'Only one small thing puzzles me. How did that pot of geraniums come to fall *upon* him rather than *with* him? But there . . .' He smiled, showing an astonishing gold tooth, 'we shall no doubt find that wind and weather had made the base unstable and that he perhaps grasped it as he fell. We do not willingly wish to embarrass our foreign visitors by trifles of this kind. *Adios, señora*, and courage.'

When he had gone we did not speak for a while. I got to my feet and went to stand by the open french window, looking out over the terrace with its bougainvillea and pots of geraniums, over the falling hillside to the far rim of the sea. I heard the police cars drive away. Pamela had stopped crying.

I turned back towards her.

'I won't tell,' I said.

She looked up. She was perfectly composed again, only the redness and moisture round her eyes showing distress. Her voice was calm. 'Tell what?'

'Look, Pamela,' I came and sat down again beside her. 'I'm on your side. You were right.'

'About what?'

'To do it. He was a shit.'

The colour came up in her face, faint under the pallor. 'You mustn't say that.'

'He was. He was a shit. Conceited, selfish, a womaniser. You know that. Dragging us all into his beastly murders. It's right, it's fitting he should die by murder, ironic really, justice.'

'Murder?'

'The police won't press it. You heard what he said. They don't want scandals in the foreign colony, its bad for tourism. We'll hear no more. But if they do come after you again, I won't say a thing. I'll absolutely deny you had any motive, any reason at all. You were right to do it, Pamela, utterly right.' I reached out and covered her hand with mine.

She looked down at them for a moment and then withdrew hers, looking up at me again with a cool, candid stare.

'Why would I want Reggie dead?' she asked.

'Why? Because he was a shit. Because of his women, the way he humiliated you, flaunted his affairs. That typist girl and Ingrid and who knows how many more. And now a servant . . .'

She said quietly, 'I didn't mind.'

'Of course you did. You couldn't not. No one would ever believe you could just go on sitting passively and let him humiliate you as he did. You'd a right to revenge.'

She got up and moved away, then turned, leaning against the fireplace where on chilly evenings a log fire used to burn. She was completely calm.

'I liked being married to Reggie,' she said, 'I liked being Mrs Reginald Tyrrell and going to parties and meeting wellknown people and living here and living in London and having money and being someone. I don't love him now like I did at first – I know he was selfish and not very nice in some ways, and all that crime and stuff sickened me often. And I didn't like some of the things he wanted me to do . . .' She blushed again, faintly, 'things in bed. I was glad when he went to other people for that. People like you.'

'Me?'

'I'm not quite a fool, Dinah. I know you've always despised me and thought I'm a nitwit. But I'm quite shrewd really, and I knew almost at once when you started sleeping with Reggie. And when he dropped you. I could see how angry you were, how ashamed and resentful, for you hadn't got anything of him, had you, while I had his name and his status and his money. I didn't want Reggie dead at all, but you did.'

There was quite a long silence after this, with us just looking at each other. Then I managed a sort of a laugh. 'What utter balls,' I said, 'As if I'd cared enough! I loathed him, I absolutely loathed him.'

'Yes,' she said, 'I know.'

There was another very long silence. I was trying to get my breath back in the same way I had tried last night when I had stood outside Reggie's french windows and steeled myself to go in. I had the perfume he liked and my hair down and only my nightgown on. I don't want to remember what I said or he said; but one of the things he said was that he'd gone past it as far as that night was concerned, no matter how much I begged, and anyway he was a bit oiled and he'd taken his sleeping pills and not even Helen of Troy or a bride in the bath could raise a flicker. I know I said, 'Only a servant, I suppose?' and I know he said something absolutely foul to me and pushed me out on to the terrace, right to the edge, and I know he had a glass in his hand and I know quite well what I decided to do, and I did it.

But it was Pamela had the motive, wasn't it, and stood to gain?

So it's stalemate really, a sort of peculiar friendship still, only it's Pamela who holds the strongest hand now. She's still Mrs

Reginald Tyrrell, attractive widow of that notable criminologist, so sadly missed and so great an authority on murder and its motives. And rich with it; Reggie was exceedingly clever with money and his books go on selling and are considered classics of their kind. Which I suppose they are.

Pamela sold the villa and we share the St John's Wood house. People often call and ask to see his Black Museum. We let them, for they're often interesting people and sometimes quite attractive. But we usually say we don't know what some of the relics are – and that includes a shard from an earthenware flower-pot with dark marks on it that might perhaps be blood. Pamela put it there.

*

Something to take back

*

While Lewis was still examining the handful of lire for a suitable tip, Betsy had crossed the room, pushed open the shutters and gone out on to the balcony.

'Oh Lewis, do look. It's heavenly!'

The shaggy tops of dark trees fell away below the hotel, pierced here and there by the pastel walls of villas, to the rippling disc of the sea. Across it a motorboat bounded; above it a small cloud composed itself agreeably in relation to the tower of the castle on the crag above the town.

'It can't be real! The blue's exactly like those butterfly-wing brooches one used to have, remember?'

He came out and stood beside her, resting his hands on the railings. 'Mm.'

She slipped her arm round his and squeezed it. 'Glad we came? Worth London Airport at three a.m.?'

'It's certainly picturesque.'

'It'll be marvellous for your sketching. And I can just bask on the beach and absolutely unwind.'

'Go easy with the sun.'

'I will. I'll do lots of shopping first – we simply mustn't leave it all till the last minute.'

He chuckled. 'You'll have to declare it all, you know.'

'Nonsense, darling – just a few little presents for the children and Mummy – and I suppose Mrs Pratt must have something. I must send them a postcard to say we've arrived.'

The railing was rough and warm under his palms. The air smelled of leaves and, faintly, cooking. Below, out of sight, there was a clatter of dishes and of conversation, too faint to be intrusive. Behind him Betsy was unpacking. Her footsteps tapped over the tiles.

'The water's marvellously hot,' she called. 'Do come and change, darling, I'm dying to get out and explore.'

The town centred round its piazza, open to the sea on one side, backed by the cathedral on the other. The hotels and most of the villas were above it, tiered up the cliffside, cushioned in foliage, reached by cobbled alleys and stairways. The beach was below it, its umbrellas a patchwork laced with limbs, on which one could gaze down over the stone wall of the piazza on the seaward side. Along this wall the town boys perched like starlings, surveying and commenting, golden in their faded T-shirts and jeans. Three or four open carriages with canopies and bedizened, dozing horses stood in the shade by the cathedral steps. On either side were cafés with bright awnings. The main street led darkly away along the cliff face, but at night it was festooned with fairy lights, as were the piazza and the trees.

'It's heavenly! It's so warm!' They had dined at the hotel and come down again to the piazza for coffee. 'Think of trying to sit in the garden at home at nine o'clock in September with only a shawl on. We must really explore tomorrow. I'll get one of those marvellous beach hats, and you must get some espadrilles, Lewis, they're terribly cheap. We might take back a pair for the children, they'd look very gay with slacks. Oh, do look at that family – the baby all starched and frilled and absolutely dropping asleep! Oh, couldn't you sketch them, darling?'

'They mightn't like it.'

'Oh, but they would!' The family had moved on, but people sauntered past endlessly, chatting and relaxed, the townspeople soberly dressed, the visitors vivid, great bronzed Scandinavians and roasted Germans, Englishmen wearing cravats, crewcut Americans, and their women with bright lips and bangles. This was a small and fashionable place, where the package tours had not yet penetrated. The quality of everything was high. The chatter of voices, the susurration of feet, the radios playing at each café, filled the bright box of the piazza.

But from their bedroom balcony the silence took over. They stood in their night-clothes looking out over the black trees to the dark sea and the star-specked infinity of sky. In the warm darkness sky, stars, sea, trees seemed to breathe like some huge watchful animal.

'There should be a moon before we leave.'

'Yes.'

'Don't get cold.'

He followed her in. 'Shall I close the shutters?'

'Well – mosquitoes, d'you think?'

'Might be. Plenty of air can get through the slats.'

'We might ask for more pillows tomorrow.'

'Would you like my dressing-gown rolled up underneath?'

'No, it's all right, darling, thank you. The mattress seems good.'

It shifted as he got in. 'D'you want to read for a bit?'

'No, I'm exhausted now. You?'

'No. It's been a long day.'

'Mm, but heavenly. It's a heavenly place.'

He switched off the light and they lay side by side on their backs, watching the dark light emerge through the slats of the shutters and the net curtains shifting in the air. He took her hand and squeezed it.

'Good night, Lewis darling. Thank you for bringing me.'

'Dear girl.' He raised himself a little to kiss her cheek, then lay back. After a moment or so they squeezed hands again and gently turned away to sleep.

'What shall we do this morning, darling? The beach?'

'Just as you like.' He fanned the first delicious, post-breakfast pipe smoke away from her.

'Do let's. The sun's so marvellous. We can buy beach hats on the way down.'

It took longer than they expected, for the choice was enormous. Almost every shop in the main street sold them and beach sandals too, shirts, shifts, scarves, dark glasses. 'Lewis, look – wouldn't one of these shirts be perfect for Tim – or even for Caroline? Such a heavenly pink! Do let's remember the shop – or, look, they've got different colours next door. How much is twelve hundred lire, Lewis?'

Eventually the hats were bought, a sort of candle-snuffer for her, a dapper panama type for him in which he looked selfconscious. He was too tall, his features too big, for so small-brimmed a hat, but it was comfortable and kept the dazzle from his eyes.

They had tickets for the beach belonging to the hotel, and an umbrella and chairs were placed for them by a smiling young man in white shorts. 'Grazie – grazie tante,' Betsy rewarded him with her special smile that was both girlish and maternal.

'Prego. Is beautiful day.'

'Ah si – beautiful.' As he moved back to the cabin she said, 'Isn't he a marvellous colour, Lewis, like dark, dark honey. Mm, isn't this heavenly!'

They took off their outer coverings, oiled themselves, stretched out. Among the tanned nakedness around them their blanched limbs looked shameful, although there were other newcomers as white. Betsy did not swim but lay in the full eye of the sun with her new hat over her face. Lewis swam, as far as the farthest raft, which was too laden with wet bodies for him to wish to board it. He turned on his back and floated, looking at the town pressed into the crevices of its mountain, crowned with the castle. He drew its shape in through his eyes to his heart; Queen Victoria Street, the office, had no meaning. For twelve days he would be an artist. The town, the cliff, the castle formed themselves into pictures as he gazed – spare, pared down pictures of forms so essential that the very soul of the place lay captured within their outlines. He swam back, dried himself, withdrew under the umbrella with a paperback. Betsy lay on her stomach now and seemed to be asleep.

After lunch they went up to their room. Betsy put on her dressing-gown and lay on the bed looking through the magazines she had bought only yesterday at London Airport. Then put them aside and closed her eyes. Lewis lay beside her, smoking his pipe. Through the wafting net curtains he could see how the light seemed to change the contours of the treetops and the crags beyond so that they stood out or receded in a way different from that of morning. He got quietly off the bed, taking the sketching-block and pencils that lay on the table. The sea sparkled, distant sounds from the town bursting like tiny fireworks in the balmy air. Yes, the castle looked quite different in this light.

'Take a chair out, darling.'

'I thought you were asleep.'

'No, only drowsing.'

'The light changes everything.' He took one of the hard chairs out on to the balcony and began to draw.

Later, wearing a different dress, showered and scented a little, she came and leaned over his shoulder.

'Mm, it's good, Lewis.'

'No – I've not got it.' He tore the drawing off the block and would have crumpled it but she took it from him.

'I think it's terribly good – all those trees, the verticals and then the shadows coming across, so – you've got the feeling.'

'No. It's a scrawl. It's more difficult than one thinks.'

'Tidy yourself up and let's go down. I'd love an ice. And I absolutely must write some postcards.'

'You go off, darling.'

'Are you sure?'

'Of course. I'll have a lovely bake and we'll meet at the café for a drink before lunch.'

'I'll come down and get you settled.'

'Don't be silly, Lewis, the boy will see to all that. It's silly to plough all the way down to the beach and then all the way up to the castle again.'

'Are you sure?'

'Darling.' She patted his cheek. 'I'm a big girl now, remember?

46

With two terrible adolescent children. Off you go and have a lovely morning.'

He took the road to begin with, but it followed the contours of the cliff too far in its ascent and he soon struck off up the rocky stairways from whose every pause new vistas of the bay and town rooftops presented themselves. In the distance goats bleated, a dog barked; flies buzzed in the shade. There was a scent of strong dark leaves and earth.

There were no cars in the open space before the castle gate and the postcard kiosk in its shade was unattended. An elderly woman in a pinafore took his fifty lire, emerging from what seemed to be her kitchen, and he passed through into the courtyard.

It was like slipping on some medieval robe, ancient and easy, of amber velvet mellowed here and there down to the weave. The blotched yellow walls were garlanded along three sides by a colonnade which on the fourth changed into a staircase leading up to a gallery on the first floor. The doors beneath the colonnade were faded and locked, and frescoes had not quite vanished from the walls – here still a halo or a benedictory hand.

Lewis went up the staircase, trailing his fingers along the warm, worn balustrade. The rooms were open off the gallery, their floors of powdery boards, their walls hung with pictures or fronted by glass cases: ivories and majolica, gilded church vessels, coins. Almost all the pictures were terrible.

These rooms were dead, but the rest of the castle lived. It was extraordinary. As he went from room to empty room or out along the crenellated walls or on to the final loggia, it was as though the generations of its owners had only that moment left by another door. The window embrasures, the battered carvings, the flaking walls and enriched ceilings were all permeated by their genial presence.

And all around, wherever one looked, the gaze soared in space. Above were nothing but the russet curled tiles of the castle and the limpid sky, beyond and below nothing but the crags, the trees, the sea marbled in turquoise and white, the tiny roofs, a cock crowing somewhere, being answered, the clatter of a pail, the union of air and skin and light and time.

He leaned for a while against the warm stone of the loggia, as every member of that household must have done throughout the centuries. Presently he began to draw.

He was late at their rendezvous, but she was later, bouncing down next to him in the chair he had with difficulty kept for her, for the cafés were all crowded at this aperitif hour. She carried her beach bag and some other packages. 'Lewis, I'm sorry, have you been waiting ages? I've bought you a Telegraph.' She smiled widely at the waiter. 'Cinzano bianco, per favore, con ice. And I did get those epadrilles for the children, red for Caroline and blue for Tim. They're just a nonsense – we'll find their real presents later on, but they're terribly cheap. How was the castle?'

'Interesting.'

'Many people?'

'No, not a soul.'

'How heavenly. The beach was packed. That nice boy who does the umbrellas speaks marvellous English, we had quite a chat. Did you do any drawings?'

'Nothing much. Nothing worth showing you.'

'I wish you drew people. The types one sees! Just look at that incredible woman – pink hair and all those dangling charms! And that absolutely heavenly man – he must be a baron, an Austrian baron!' Through the crowd and dominating it as much by his bearing as by his height, moved an unmistakably Nordic man, his middle-age varnished with a golden tan, hair golden and smooth, muscles taut beneath the golden hairs, a blue silk shirt, blue jeans, and round the wrist a linked gold bracelet. Two young men, as dark as he was fair, elbowed beside him through the crowd, two row-boats in the wake of an iceberg.

Lewis finished his drink. 'Consenting adults, I think.'

'Oh Lewis!' She pressed his arm reprovingly. 'D'you really think so? What a waste!'

48

She slept that afternoon, while Lewis went back again up the hillside. Later she went out on to the hotel terrace to wait for him to join her, watching the swift dusk muffle the trees and the sea, and the lights come on in the town and among the vines and pergolas of the terrace. From the bar came the sound of music, interspersed with the patter of radio commercials, and the quiet hum of voices. Other guests came out on to the terrace, spruce and ready for the evening, couples like herself and Lewis, well dressed, easy in circumstance, with grown or growing children back home in England, Germany, Sweden or the United States. They did not speak to her, as she was a woman alone; and she did not speak to them, for it was not to meet people like themselves that she and Lewis had found their way to Santa Felicia.

The sea was gone now. One sharp star showed in the indigo sky. She sat waiting for Lewis.

'You go, darling – honestly.'

'You're sure?'

'Darling, you don't really like baking, do you and I'm determined to lose this terrible British pallor. I'll have a good bake and then I really must try and find something for Mummy, I've not seen a thing yet that would really do. You go, I want you to.'

So he went, not direct to the castle today, but following paths along the hillside, between the trees and the brilliant sea, always with new visions that he tried to cage between pencilled lines.

And she went down to the beach, where the bodies and umbrellas were already spread, smiling Buon giorno to Giorgio, the beach boy, who later, when she had sunbathed and was sitting back under the shade, came by and spoke to her.

'Is beautiful day, signora.'

'Si, beautiful. Every day is beautiful here.'

'You like the sun?'

'Very much.'

'Your husband not so much, I think.'

'No, not so much. He has a sensitive skin.'

'So he not come to the beach.'

'No. He likes to draw, too – an artist, you know, pictures?'

'Ah, artist.'

'Yes. He's up at the castello now, making pictures.'

'He makes pictures for money?'

'Heavens no! We shouldn't be able to come here if he did that! No, he's just an amateur. It's his hobby, you know – he just does it for fun.'

'Ah, si.' He nodded his glossy head.

'He's very good,' she said sternly, 'Very good. We always use one of his drawings as Christmas cards.'

'He make picture of you?' His gaze encompassed her.

'No, not people. Places only, buildings – you know?'

'Ah si, capisco.'

She began packing up the beach bag. 'I must go and do some shopping. Perhaps you can advise me which is the best shop for gifts, souvenirs?'

'Alessandrini's in the main street, signora – very good, very cheap.'

'They speak English?'

'Si, si – is my sister. Say Giorgio send you, she make special price.'

'How marvellous.'

'Permesso, signora,' He took the beach bag and they walked between the bodies up to the cabin.

'Thank you so much.'

'Prego, signora.'

'Ciao, then . . .'

'Ciao.' His smile was like a toothpaste advertisement, he moved with the grace of a well-oiled, warm statue. Alain Delon, she thought, climbing the steps, and Tim when he was still a little boy . . .

She bought several things at Alessandrini's, including a silk shirt for herself, but she still could find nothing really right for her mother. As for Mrs Pratt, she would probably like one of those rather awful ceramics, a vase or a couple of tiles for the teapot or something, but those could be bought later on. There were some rather sweet little earrings made of shells, pure kitsch of course, but terribly pretty; she bought a pair for Caroline and another for herself, and put hers on, under the cherishing encouragement of Giorgio's sister.

She was too early for Lewis, who would probably be late, so she crossed the baking centre of the piazza and leaned her elbows on the wall above the beach. Even through her sunglasses the light was dazzling, the wavelets and the rocks seeming to strike sparks from one another, the brown naked people glowing, the floats skating about among the swimmers and the air echoing with their voices. A little along the wall three or four town boys lounged. They eyed her, joking among themselves, but in a way which did not seem to her offensive. They were youths only, hardly older than Timothy, they would have no interest in someone old enough to be their mother; yet their eyes and the tone of their voices were pleasing, even if she was glad she could not understand what they were saying. Of course, with her sunglasses on, her slenderness and her pretty earrings, they could take her for much younger than she was. But that was the marvellous thing about Italians – they sort of paid homage to your basic femininity, whatever your age. They saw past the birthdays and the now slightly unresilient flesh to the woman within, more desirable now, riper, than a girl. They respected Woman; whatever the quips being exchanged along the wall, the young men's eyes were, in their own funny way, terribly respectful. Like Giorgio's.

After lunch, after a little while, she called from the bed to Lewis as he sat reading on the balcony. 'Aren't you coming to lie down, darling?'

'I thought you'd dropped off.'

'No, I'm not sleepy. You?'

'No. Sleeping in the daytime always gives me a headache. There's a nice breeze out here.'

After a moment she swung her feet down from the bed. 'What would you like to do?'

He closed the book, marking the place with a cypress frond he had brought down from the hillside. 'The beach?'

'It's too hot in the afternoon.'

'We could go for a jaunt?'

'They've probably all left by now. Take me up to your castle.'

'If you like. It's quite a pull.'

'I don't mind – you say there's a breeze.'

They set off. She picked a spray of bougainvillea and tucked it in the buttonhole of his shirt, and pulled a twig of some sweet-scented shrub and sniffed its leaves. The lanes were agreeable, dappled with shade, but the paths beyond them were certainly steep, their flagged steps spaced an awkward pace and a half so that she must go up in a stride or else dot-and-carry. In the open stretches the sun blazed, in the shade flies fastened in swarms. When they emerged by the castle its gate was obscured by two charabancs, the building itself entirely overrun by hearty Germans.

He had found a little lane that ran round the outside of the castle walls and along this he led her until they reached a place where flattish rocks made it possible to sit. He lit his pipe to keep the flies away, saying, between puffs, 'Sorry about the coach party.'

'Oh – you weren't to know.'

'Tired?'

'I'd love a drink.'

'We might be able to get something at the kiosk.'

'I'd rather wait till we get back.'

He puffed, gazing out over the sea.

'Does this path lead anywhere?'

'I suppose it must do. Everything has a purpose up here, tracks for goats or carts, to farms or to the next village.'

'Imagine it in the winter!'

He glanced at her, then put his arm round her shoulders. 'I warned you it was a pull.'

'Lewis . . .' She lay against him, then raised her hand and bent

52

his head towards hers. He removed the pipe from his mouth with his free hand and kissed her. She stroked the back of his neck. 'Lewis . . .'

'Darling girl.' He kissed her again, twice. She put her other arm across his body and rested her head against his neck. He replaced the pipe in his mouth and stroked her arm. It was very peaceful. The flies buzzed. Presently they both had pins and needles, and got up to walk the easier way down.

That night as they lay hand in hand Lewis turned towards her, kissed her cheek. 'Betsy?'

'Yes.'

He kissed her again, gently. 'Have you . . . ?'

'Yes.'

The moves were no less dear for being familiar; no less familiar for being made in the dusk of an Italian bedroom, against pillows with a different angle, bedboards at a different length, mattress with different springs. There was no strangeness, and no revelation. As always, he was silent, revealing nothing. As always, she hardly knew when it began or ended. They exchanged small kisses, like children, afterwards, and went to sleep turned, as always, back to back.

Betsy did not visit the castle again. They made a little joke about 'Castello Luigi' and 'Betsy's Grill', and every morning it was accepted that after breakfast he should take his sketching things and go up the hillside and she should take her beach bag and go down to the beach. Often he went back again after lunch, while she rested, although sometimes they went on excursions: by car along the cliff road to neighbouring towns or in a motorboat across to the further arm of the bay.

Every morning when Giorgio saw her coming alone down the steps behind the cabins he would hasten to take her bag from her and escort her to her place, open the umbrella, set the deck chair, then go away to do the same for someone else. She would slip off her beach dress, oil herself, put on her sunglasses, spread the towel and lie down in the sun which every day grew in the same glory towards midday. With her eyes shut the voices and movements around her were dimmed, and thoughts small as minnows idled in and out of the recesses of her mind. She still hadn't found the right present for Mummy – or for Lewis, come to that . . . Or, increasingly, in fancy she continued the scene with Giorgio: he would stretch out beside her, Our Italian sun suits you signora, Why yes Giorgio I could lie in it for ever, I too signora, a long look from his boy's eyes, gentle laughter, Why Giorgio you're too young just to lie in the sun, Yes only to lie, signora . . .

The day after she had been to the castle, the day after she and Lewis had made love, as a cross in her diary testified (a record she had started in her child-bearing days) she had seen Giorgio stripped to his bathing-trunks. She had been aware of laughter and Italian voices back in the cabin and had opened her eyes at the thud of feet running past her to see Giorgio and two other young men romping their way down to the water and hurtling into it to swim a mad race, wrestle and dive, surface and speed on, their torsos golden in the blue water, their heads black as dolphins, to wade out on to the beach at last, laughing and dripping, and run wrestling again up the beach out of sight.

She had lain down and shut her eyes again, suffused with lust. It beat up against all reason: he was a beach boy, the same age as her son, he had no eyes for women old enough to be his mother, there must be many middle-aged English women who deluded themselves . . . The gold-muscled flesh . . . This was ridiculous, shameful. Yet what harm could it do? No one but she knew what she was thinking, she hardly knew herself. Stretched in the sun, not old yet, shapely in her moulded bathing-dress, a woman who had lain with a man the night before . . . The flesh, with the sun sparkling through the dark hairs, the nakedness . . .

So each morning she lay on the beach, prolonging, sometimes in fancy, sometimes in fact, her conversation with Giorgio. And his eyes did linger, his fingers did occasionally rest on hers as he took her bag from her; as he exchanged the trivialities which were their conversation his voice did warm them into something

intimate, something secret shared between them and acknowl-
edged in the ardour of his beautiful eyes and the answer she
sometimes allowed to flash from hers.

During the siesta hours, with Lewis either absent or reading on
the balcony, she shut herself within her closed eyelids and
fantasied. It was ridiculous; she knew it; it meant nothing, was of
no importance. No one would ever know, even she would forget,
when they had left this sunny, voluptuous place which existed
only for the senses. The days were passing, soon the holiday
would be over. She still had shopping to do, still had no present
for Mummy or a proper one for Tim, still had to go through the
address book for people they must send cards to, and only a few
more days. She had a hairdresser's appointment for the day after
her return; and must send Tim's shoes to be mended and slacks
to be cleaned before he went back to Keele. Mrs Pratt would want
a week off with pay, a reward for holding the fort. The winter
curtains must go up. She must think what to wear for Lewis's
partners' annual cocktail party . . . A tap on the door, Who is it? It
is I, Giorgio. Giorgio? You left your sunglasses on the beach,
signora, How kind of you to bring them, Not kind signora, I could
not help it, Not help it why Giorgio, Signora signora . . . hands,
mouth, thighs . . .

'Lewis, I'm getting rather desperate.'

'Mm?'

'I simply can't find anything for Mummy. I've looked and
looked in all the shops and there just doesn't seem anything that's
exactly right.'

He took a sip of Carpano. 'You might find something in Porta
Fiorita. We'll take the bus there tomorrow if you like.'

'I looked when we were there, there was simply nothing. I
suppose I could get Tim a really good tie, but his lot don't seem to
wear them any more.'

'Haven't you got him that sports shirt?'

'Yes, but that's not enough. We must take more than just

one thing back with us for them. There are only three more days.'

'What about a cameo for your mother?'

'She hates them. And they're not very good here really, unless you pay a lot.'

'We'd better go in to dinner.'

'You're not being very constructive, are you?'

'What d'you expect me to do? I've suggested going to Porta Fiorita again. You always make such a performance of taking presents home.'

'Well, you don't do it, do you? You leave it all to me.'

He followed her into the hotel. 'We'll have another look round the town this evening then. Good God, the whole main street's nothing but tourist traps, there must be something.'

So they patrolled the town again, looking at wares they had already looked at, buying a few small things that left the main problem unsolved. Afterwards, when they sat in the piazza, she kept looking for Giorgio among the crowds, some of whom had by now become familiar: the woman with pink hair and her noisy friends, an elderly couple who never spoke to each other, the exquisite Nordic baron and his catamites. Inside each café music of some sort was playing, mingling in the coffee-scented air with the voices and the shuffling feet of the promenaders, among whom the town boys lounged, sharp-eyed, sharp-tongued. But Giorgio did not appear.

They were flying home on Sunday night, and on Saturday there was to be a concert in the piazza and the castle would be floodlit. 'They put flambeaux in the courtyard, the old woman at the gate told me. The place must come completely alive.'

'How weird. I wonder it doesn't burn down.'

'It's survived – or parts of it – for close on a thousand years.'

'And you've immortalised it in your sketches.' Her smile was affectionate, but her tone was not. 'When are you going to let me see them?'

He knocked out the dottle of his post-breakfast pipe, felt for his penknife and began cleaning the bowl. 'When we leave.'

'You've never been so secretive.'

'It's more difficult than other places I've done. There's a quality – don't you feel it?'

'I know what you mean, of course.' Her gaze wandered down towards the sea and she got to her feet. 'Why don't you go up there tonight, see your flambeaux?'

'I couldn't leave you on your own, our last evening.'

'Don't be silly, darling. We can go to the concert and you can bring me back and then plod on upwards to your dream castello.'

'No, no . . .' But his gaze strayed upward, as hers had downward, as they went indoors before separating for the morning.

'Almost my last morning, Giorgio.'

'Ah, che peccato!'

'We go home tomorrow evening.'

'Is sad. Many peoples go home now, is end of season.'

'Yes, the end of the season.'

'You will miss the sun, signora.'

'I shall miss many things.'

'I too.'

'I shall miss coming out on the balcony every morning and looking at the sea.'

'Is beautiful view. You are which hotel?'

She busied herself with the beachbag. 'The Miramare. On the second floor. You can see the balcony from here, the one on the end, the end room.'

He shaded his eyes to look upward. 'Ah, si – where the yellow towel hangs?'

'Yes. My husband likes to sit there when he's not up at the castello. But he usually goes. In the afternoons I have a siesta and he goes to the castello. He's going up there tonight too, after the concert.'

'So? He like the castello very much?'

'Very much.'

She looked at him and he looked back at her, smiling and easy, the sun sheening his glossy hair and the glossy flesh of his arms. In a silence that she felt must burst, she turned away and put on her sunglasses, for she could not accept the inscrutability of his eyes or the declaration in her own.

'Allora – then I will say arrivederci, signora.'

'Arrivederci, Giorgio.'

Lewis went back to the castle immediately after lunch, pausing in their bedroom no longer than was necessary to repoint his pencils and put a new and differently surfaced sketching-pad into his portfolio.

'Have a good session, Lewis.'

'Yes. I'll be back as usual.'

He left. He might have been going to the office. She took off her dress and slip. Beneath them in this warm land she wore only a bra and briefs. She put on her dressing-gown, ruffled and rosy and impractical, re-did her face, brushed out her hair; put perfume between her breasts, plumped up in their lacy container. She lay down on the bed. Sounds from the town came up remotely through the latched shutters, the muslin curtains stirred. The afternoon was brilliant outside; in here all was dusk and stillness, fragrance and languor. She watched the curtains and the bright afternoon between the slats. Her thoughts stopped.

She got up around five and opened the shutters. The glare had gone and the sea had turned to silk. She must, she supposed, have slept. She turned back into the room. Presently, showered, changed and freshly groomed, she sat waiting for Lewis on the hotel terrace, turning a glass of Cinzano between her fingers, watching the lights come on in the town.

'How did it go?'

'So-so. I somehow can't . . . If you really don't mind, dear, I think I will go back this evening.'

'Do.'

'I can't . . . I'd like to see it as it used to be.'

'Of course.' A nerve of imagination began to tick again. 'You go. It will probably look marvellous.'

'Why don't you come? We could take a taxi up.'

'No, I'll be tired. I've got packing to do. I'd rather go to bed.'

At nine o'clock the concert began. A platform had been erected at one side of the piazza, garlanded with paper flowers, and on it a brass band played Rossini, excerpts from Turandot, and the whole of Beethoven's Fifth Symphony. 'It's not possible!' whispered Betsy; but it was. She and Lewis were squeezed at a table almost in the middle of the piazza, for the cafés had flooded out and filled it with their furniture; there was hardly room to walk between the chairs. All along the sea wall, all up the steps of the cathedral and the sloping entrances to the alleyways, the townspeople squatted or stood, not more silent but more attentive than the visitors, applauding each item with large-palmed warmth and cries of 'Bravi!' Above the crowded glitter of the piazza a half-formed moon now hung in the huge sky, and above that, it seemed, as remote and golden-pearly, hung the floodlit castle, its walls and turrets ghostly in the darkness, an inner shimmer from the torches within its courtyard making it seem to float and waver like a mirage.

The garish clamour, the crowds, the caressing air were like pulses beating inside Betsy. On every side people with naked limbs were clinging, laughing, being together. They had all made love that afternoon in their dim-shuttered rooms, or would make love that night, the music still in their veins; in all the villas and hotels, cities of bedrooms with cool floors and pillows, people coupled, behind every closed door, every papered wall, above every ceiling, husbands or lovers, some long known but some found here, growth of this place, this sensuous living dream. She had forgotten Lewis, as he had forgotten her. He stared up from the clamour around him to the castle, palely haunting the sky. The sunlight had been impersonal; under it the castle smiled but did not speak. But by torchlight it would speak, its shadows peopled. It would breathe again under the timeless flicker of the flambeaux, re-creating itself in his sight. And he would enter it.

And Betsy looked up too but to the hotel, to the shadowed balconies with their shutters linked close by the maids, their sheets turned back and opening the beds, the pillows waiting. And she looked round over the crowd, searching the cathedral steps, the wall, the alley mouths, scheming to pass her message by a look, to leave this place, be rid of Lewis, enclose herself in the quiescent darkness of the bedroom till the door opened softly and Giorgio lay with her.

The concert ended, with the Valkyrie, many 'Bravissimas' and a sheaf of gladioli for the conductor. The peripheral crowd broke up, the café tables began to empty a little.

'Had enough?' She nodded, drawing her shawl tightly round her shoulders. 'Let's move then.'

They got up.

As they made their way through the tables they saw the Nordic baron. His fair hair smooth as a helmet, his tanned face impassive, he sat at a table near the trees, the gold bracelet glinting on his tanned arm as he played idly with the dark nape of the youth beside him, who arched his neck a little at the touch, smiling, smoking an American cigarette.

Of course it was Giorgio.

Lewis did not go up to the castle that evening after all. It was not like Betsy to cry, and although she insisted it was the result of too much sun on 'Betsy's Grill', he felt it was more than that. It had started when they got inside their door. He made her go to bed, and brought cold compresses with which he gently wiped her face, her brow that had always had lines on it, even as a girl, her eyes that so often were gay and teasing now puffy and red with crying. She lay on her back, quiet at last save for an occasional catch of the breath, and he sat on the bed beside her holding her hand in both his. Presently he put it aside. 'I'll get you a sleeping-pill.'

'Must I?'

'I should.' He found the bottle, shook one out, fetched water. She raised herself on one elbow and drank it down. 'Good girl.'

'I ought to do some packing.'

'Not tonight. We'll do it together in the morning.'

60

She lay down again while he took the glasses back to the alcove and then began to undress. 'I'll have to get a cameo for Mummy after all.'

'They're quite handsome.'

'And they are local. Have we got enough left for a good one?'

'I think so.'

'And I will get Tim a tie. Caro's done.'

'Mrs Pratt?'

'A horrible vase – just right.'

He chuckled, tying the cord of his pyjamas. 'D'you want to read a bit?'

'No. The pill's beginning to work.'

He went to the window. 'Shall we have the shutters open tonight and risk mosquitoes?'

'Yes let's – our last night.'

'Turn off the lamp first, then.'

She did so.

He opened the shutters and stepped out on to the balcony. All but the main town lights had been turned off, and there was no sound; only a sense of movement out of sight, of the sea stirring, the stars and shadow moon arching; the smell of night. When he looked up towards the castle he could not see it, for the flood-lighting had ended.

They spent the last morning shopping – there was no Sunday closing during the season. They got the cameo brooch and the tie, and a pair of expensive shoes for Betsy, a present from Lewis. She had already given him a leather wallet and, tucked inside it as a joke, a town badge which showed the castle machine-embroidered in yellow on an electric-blue silk background. They had a last drink in the piazza and went back to the hotel to pack.

'Where's the portfolio, Lewis?'

'Here.'

'It looks very thin.' She opened it. 'Darling, where are they all?'

'What?'

'Your sketches.'

'They weren't any good.'

'You haven't destroyed them?'

'They were no good.'

'Lewis?' She pressed the portfolio to her, staring at him aghast. 'When?'

'Last night, when you were asleep.'

'Oh Lewis, how could you! All those hours and hours – and nothing, in the end, nothing to show for it.'

'I just couldn't get it, somehow. There was a quality . . . The old boys could do it – there are some little drawings up there in the museum, tucked away – they'd got it all right.'

'But, Lewis, I'm sure yours were good.'

'Not good enough. I've learned that anyway.'

'Oh darling – and you loved it so! And no Christmas card!'

'Time for a change.'

'Wait, though . . .' She put the portfolio down and went to her suitcase, drawing from the flap inside the lid the sketch he had done the day after they arrived. 'There – I've saved something! What luck!'

'Let me see.'

He took the drawing from her. The tentative pencil marks were too weak to enclose form; their accuracy held no truth, their shading no bulk, their lines no feeling. It said nothing, revealed nothing save a niggling verisimilitude. It was the work of an amateur with little talent.

She took it back from him. 'I shall certainly use it for the card, it's very good. Besides, we must have something to take back.'

*

Juno's swans

*

So: the last of England. But I am not one of Mr Ford Madox
Brown's hollow-eyed consumptives, nor do I have some pallid
virgin clinging to my arm, the very picture of wan defeat. Leaning
on the rail of this P and O steamship, I confess to a singular
satisfaction as I watched the murky shores of my homeland
recede. I have done with her, with everything that held me there. I
have no ties. I shall occupy my time on shipboard very tolerably.
No doubt there will be whist; I shall make my regular perambula-
tions round the deck morning and afternoon; I shall, if requested,
contribute a dramatic monologue to the ship's concert; I shall
devote my civilities to mature ladies travelling under the protection of their husbands and to young ladies travelling under that of
their mamas. A man of intelligence – and I flatter myself I am far
from being a fool – will hardly put his head into the same noose
twice.

So here I am, ensconced in the solitude of the Writing Room,
feeling the ship begin its slow plunge and rise as we move into
open water, hearing the footsteps and voices of the other passengers as they bustle up and down the passageways, exploring the
mighty monster that will be their home and haven for so many
weeks before we reach Bombay. In an hour or two the dinner bell
will sound. Until then it amuses me to sit here undisturbed and to
commit to the thick sheets of steamship notepaper, handsomely
embossed with pennants and anchors, the singular events which
led me to leave my native shores. England, farewell! To para-
phrase Cardinal Wolsey, Farewell, a long farewell to all my
weakness!

I first met Emmeline at the house of mutual friends in Portman

Square. It was a musical evening and I had been prevailed upon, after the tenors and sopranos had been heard, to give my rendering of Mr Irving's famous soliloquy from 'The Bells'. I confess I do it well – I was a leading light in my University theatricals, and no doubt it was my histrionic bent which led me to read for the Bar, although happily I have never been required to earn my living from it. The Bar or the pulpit are the only alternatives to a gentleman with a talent for drama, and I had no taste for the pulpit.

When my recitation ended I was surrounded by a host of cooing ladies: So powerful, so tragic, so thrilling, quite blood-curdling! And when the tide of lace, ribbons and flounces had receded I found my hand encased by the small kid-gloved fingers of a girl, fair and pale as a fairy, small as an elf, who stared up at me with great violet eyes. 'You will haunt my dreams,' she said in a sighing sort of voice.

An elderly gent, fat and purple of jowl, thrust up behind her. 'Capital, capital! Better than the Lyceum, I assure you!'

'You're too kind,' I said, or something of the sort.

'Not a bit of it, sir. Capital, quite striking!'

The young lady had released my hand and stood now with downcast eyes, playing with her fan.

'I trust I shall not seriously disturb this young lady's dreams,' I said. 'I have no desire to be a bogeyman.'

'What? Bogeyman? Nonsense, sir, nonsense! Too fanciful, Emmeline – my daughter, sir, and I am Colonel . . .' well, it doesn't matter who. Within six months he was dead, struck down by an apoplexy, which was not surprising considering his size and the amount of brandy he poured into himself. A decent old codger, though, who took me to his heart for dual reasons: firstly, he had no son and, like all military men, regretted it. Although I am far from being the kind of fellow such a man might be thought to have admired (for I abhor your bluff, hard-drinking Service type whose only talk is whores and horses) I was in fact, I surmise, what he would secretly have liked as a son. I am tall, elegant, handsome – no need for false modesty here. I do not bluster or

64

guffaw, my control is perfect, yet my histrionic talent shows that I am capable of feeling.

His second reason, without doubt, was the desire to see his daughter safely married and to someone in whom he had perfect confidence. She was something of an heiress; but that, he soon found out, was immaterial to me, since I have ample means of my own. She was also delicate; her mother had died a few years after her birth (which had no doubt accelerated an inevitable decline) and Emmeline had inherited a constitutional weakness which made her frail as a flower and sometimes as beautiful. Her father, good old man, was anxious that she should not wed some coarse-grained fellow who would wear her out with child-bearing but someone who would cherish and encourage her frail energies and bring her the tranquillity she needed.

Such a man was myself. I am not a sensual man. I won't deny that I have, from time to time in my youth, patronised the better houses of Mayfair or kept a dollymop for a month or two in some discreet Kensington villa; but the gross beauties of the Haymarket were not for me, I have ever been far too fastidious, too elevated in spirit to wallow, as my fellow students did, in the stews and taverns of the metropolis.

There was something about Emmeline to which this delicacy in my nature responded. She was small and frail, with fair hair that curled and fronded over her white brow and those great violet eyes. Her skin was pale and gauzy, like the wings one almost thought to see at her shoulders as, when she was in health, she flitted here and there about the house and grounds of . . . let us call it Haylett Hall. She was like some fragile flower that too easily wilts and fades, but, like them, she could revive and bloom again after some days of rest, her light, breathless voice trilling once more through the panelled rooms and passages of the house.

She aroused in me a singular mixture of emotions: a masculine instinct to protect and dominate, a curiosity as to the essence of her charm, something of a collector's pleasure in a rare and delicate piece, the pleasure of possession. Her white and childlike beauty attracted me strongly.

I had asked the Colonel for her hand two months after our meeting. He had embraced me, the engagement was announced, the wedding date arranged, and then he died. Amidst our tears we decided to continue as had been planned, for it was what he would have wished and the wedding was in any event to be a quiet one in the village church close by the Hall.

Thus it was. A brief honeymoon at Broadstairs (we did not venture abroad, for Emmeline dreaded the sea) and we returned to Haylett Hall to start our new life together – as had been planned from the beginning, for we would have lived as son and daughter with the Colonel, had he been spared.

Haylett Hall is not large but it is commodious and it is beautiful. Built in the reign of Charles the Second, it has undergone various additions and enrichments, mainly in the time of George the Fourth. It has been in Emmeline's family for some two hundred years and the gardens, parkland and the strange wild area known as the Workings have been enlarged and beautified over that period. It was property to be proud of and I was proud of it – indeed, it is perhaps the only single thing that I regret leaving behind me.

We settled in. It seemed a perfect life. I did not regret relinquishing my barrister's chambers, since I hardly practised. We had an ample circle of acquaintances within the neighbourhood, a well-trained staff of servants – and Sybil.

Sybil. I confess I have paused in my narrative a while after writing that name. Sybil. As dark as Emmeline was fair, almost as tall as I, slender and swift as a sword. Sybil.

Of course I had known about Sybil. I had met her whenever I visited Haylett Hall to pay my addresses to Emmeline, and had escorted the two of them on their calls about the county. The two girls had been friends from childhood, had grown up together under the Colonel's care when Sybil's parents were tragically murdered by tribesmen near Kabul – the two men were brother officers and friends. It was Sybil who ran the household, who cared for Emmeline when she was ill, who nursed the old man through his final days. Something between an elder sister and a

66

companion, she was as much a part of the house, I soon came to understand, as the panelling itself or the dark portraits on the stairs; and like them she did not obtrude herself, but seemed to be always there should she be needed, discreetly absent so that Emmeline and I could be alone during our courtship, present again for a hand of whist, a tramp over the countryside, an evening's laughter and song round the piano in the large, log-lit drawing room. As strong as Emmeline was weak, she was an ever-present part of life at Haylett Hall, watchful for our comfort, a smile ever hovering on her lips, her dark eyes ever alert.

When the old man had died, and Emmeline lay prostrate in her room, tear-stained and weak with grief, Sybil had come to me as I sat before the fire in the library, musing on the enigma of mortality. Her eyes were red but there was no weakness in her manner. Direct as always, she said, 'Gerald,' she said, 'I hope you will not postpone the wedding.'

I murmured that I had not so intended.

'I'm glad,' she said, clasping her long hands nervously so that the chatelaine she wore at her belt swung and tinkled against her skirt. 'It will be best for Emmeline. With the Colonel gone, she may so easily decline. She needs a man's authority to order her affairs, to hold her grasp on life. My care for her is not enough.'

'I swear solemnly that mine shall be.'

'Yes.' She looked at me, direct and dark. 'Yes, that is what I believe. It is for her sake, you see. It is what is best for her.' She turned and left the room. We never spoke of it again.

So we were man and wife, Emmeline and I. My flower, my fairy was mine, we talked and ate, played music and cards together, walked a little if the weather were fine, not too far and not too fast, drove out in the carriage, well wrapped up with rugs, went to London for a few weeks in the season if she were up to it, leaving Sybil at home. We shared a life together, Emmeline and I; but it was not a married life.

I need not be too delicate. Who, after all, will read this tale but I? That fairy, that gossamer girl who had so entranced and intrigued my senses, was no more a woman than is a whiting upon the fishmonger's slab. I am not, as I have said, a sensual man. I can forgo the pleasures of the flesh without inconvenience if circumstances order it. But marriage postulates certain activities, certain rights, and these not only was my poor Emmeline quite ignorant of but cringed from when the facts were known.

For some months I persevered, but although I conquered her resistance I never overcame her horror of this natural act – no doubt her terror of childbirth played some part in this, one must be charitable. Whatever the causes, connubial life with Emmeline soon became at first a mockery, then a penance, finally nothing. I moved out of the matrimonial bedroom into a handsome room the other side of the house, drawing on all my resources of fortitude and self-sufficiency to build a tolerable life of my own, as indifferent as I could make myself to the twittering, childish ninny I had somehow married and who was rapidly (due, no doubt, to the lengthening periods spent bed-ridden or lying upon sofas in a perhaps unconscious retreat from her obligations) growing fat.

I will not dwell upon that period of my life. Schooled in self-discipline though I am, even now I can scarce control the bitter anger, the resentment of those days, denied the comforts to which I had the right, including that of children. All men desire a son. I won't pretend I care much for children, with their squalls and squabbles (I trust there aren't too many aboard this ship) but I had the right to expect my name, my talents and my handsome figure to be perpetuated. Well, no matter . . .

I lived sufficient to myself, affable to my neighbours, courteous to my wife, cold behind a mask of polite indifference. But slowly, more and more – Sybil.

My eyes were drawn to her when she was present, my thoughts when she was absent. Slowly she possessed first my waking reveries, then my dreams – dreams such as I had never experienced before. In them she was half naked, her slender body maddeningly revealed through torn or opened garments, shameless, lewd . . . In my dreams she spoke words from the gutter, made gestures from the stews. She drew me on, shuddering, wild . . . and in the morning I would look at her, neat and bright in her sensible country clothes, pouring the coffee, passing the kedgeree, adjusting Emmeline's rug, putting the slippers on those useless feet, holding the cup while she drank, gently brushing back that frizzing hair – and my eyes would burn at her over that mockery and she would meet my gaze, direct, bright, then turn aside to tend yet further the soft pale slug our fairy had become.

Sometimes, if Emmeline were well enough to come downstairs, I would find Sybil's gaze fixed upon me over the couch where my wife lay. Sometimes our hands would touch, she withdrawing hers with a swift movement and averted eyes. She kept more and more to Emmeline's rooms, but when we encountered one another her eyes sought mine again, dark, burning, questing. Once, when the doctor had just taken his leave after Emmeline had suffered one of her collapses, we stood at the foot of the stairs together, she almost as tall as I, her pale red-mouthed face lamp-lit, her eyes brilliant. She laid a hand on my arm and said, her voice trembling, 'She is suffering, Gerald.'

I covered her hand with mine and dared to say, 'We are all suffering here.'

'Yes. Yes, that's true.' She withdrew her hand, glancing nervously at the parlourmaid who passed down the hall after seeing the doctor out. So low I could hardly hear her, she said, 'I can't bear to see her suffer.'

She turned and went swiftly up the stairs, back to Emmeline's side, holding her long skirts in one delicate hand, the white neck bent under the dark knot of hair that in my dreams had been so wild, so tangled. Watching her go, I said in my heart, You shall not, dearest. We will suffer no more.

I don't propose to go in detail into what followed. The practicalities are tedious and unimportant. Suffice it to say that it is uncommonly easy to obtain arsenic in sufficient quantities to kill an army, if you declare it is an army of rats, that no name I ever gave any chemist astute enough to desire one was ever verified, and that if one's purchases are made sufficiently far afield there is singularly little chance that anyone will ever recognise one. Add to all this a trusting domestic staff, a show of concern and husbandly attention, patience and common sense, and you will readily understand how Emmeline's illness, slight at first following that collapse, increased to a distressing and ultimately fatal conclusion. She was only twenty-eight.

Sybil was prostrated. We all were. The maids crept about red-eyed and snivelling, the butler and my own man looked grave as undertakers, the neighbours called dripping crape and condolences. I kept to my room for twenty-four hours, for truth to tell the event had taken its toll of me. When I issued forth again I was astonished at my haggard appearance, pale and distinguished like the Commendatore's ghostly statue in Don Juan. I went about the sad business attendant upon death, mourned with the doctor over madeira and biscuits in the darkened library, accepted his regrets that medical skill, alas . . . and was afire for Sybil. Her maid told me she was prostrated still. The doctor prescribed sleeping draughts. I paced the silent house and empty gardens, wild with impatience to see that lovely form appear, pale and tear-stained though she needs must be, sad too at the passing of a childhood friend, but looking at me with that clear bright gaze, the dark hair burning from the high brow, the slender figure vibrant . . .

Behind my grave composure I was mad with longing. My dreams mingled with my yearning till I felt I must rush and beat upon her door, throw myself in upon her, on her'. . . I held myself rigid, schooled and disciplined to the outside world, a flawless performance. I sat, I waited; I walked, and waited. At last she came.

It was at the Workings, that wilderness of wood and quarry, of tangled bushes and treacherous paths where they say ancient Britons delved for flint, thick with trees and undergrowth now down its steep sides, with the glimpse of stagnant water at the bottom where once men had hacked at the rock. There is a path along the top, heavy with blackberries and foxgloves in their season, and at its curve a wooden seat, for the prospect opens out just there and you can see across the quarry to the hills beyond the

70

village, the far side of the valley. It was the afternoon before the funeral and I had fled the house and my intolerable waiting, had taken a walking-stick and slashed my way through the wood to the Workings path and the bench, and there Sybil was sitting. She was weeping, her head in its simple bonnet bent into her hands, the veil thrown back. She started to her feet as I appeared.

'Gerald!'

'My dearest!' It burst from me in a groan and I held out my arms to her. She came into them like a bird, quivering and sobbing. I felt her slender body against mine, strong and smooth and so wonderfully alive. I took the bonnet gently from her head and dropped it on the bench, smoothed the hair from her wet cheeks. 'Sybil,' I said, 'Sybil . . .'

'Oh Gerald . . .' She lifted her head and looked at me, eyes drenched in tears. 'Oh Gerald, what shall I do? How can I bear it?'

'Hush, my dearest, we will bear it together. It is my burden rather than yours.'

'No, no, it is mine.' She pushed herself free and took a few steps away. 'You don't know – you can't know. What can my life be now?'

I stepped forward and took her hand. 'Your life will be with me, Sybil. In a little while, when a decent interval has passed. With me, Sybil, with me . . .' I covered her hand with kisses.

'What?' She stared at me and stepped backwards, pulling her hand away. 'What are you saying?'

'That I love you, Sybil. I have longed to say it for months, years, to shout it aloud, to breathe it in your ears. I have longed to say it with my lips, to hear you say it with yours rather than with your eyes, your burning, brilliant eyes . . .'

'You are mad!' she cried.

'With love, with longing! Sybil . . .' I seized her hand again, striving to draw her to me once more and kiss at last that red, red mouth.

With violent strength she thrust me from her. 'You are mad!' she repeated. 'Mad! What fantasy is this?'

'No fantasy but a dream dreamed by us both. I saw it in your

71

voice, your eyes. While she lived we were mute, but now . . . My dearest, my only passionate love . . .'

With all her strength she struck me across the face. She was breathing fast, her eyes wildly blazing, her voice shrill. 'You fool!' she cried. 'You mad, evil fool! I never loved you, I could never love you! It was she I loved, she, she, my silver flower, my gentle, tender woman – only she, only she . . .' She began to weep again.

I stared at her. 'You loved my wife?'

'Yes, yes, always! It was only she . . .'

'You loved her – as I love you?'

'More, much more. What can men know of love . . .'

I struck her. She was near the edge, and she fell.

After a while the bushes were silent again, the stagnant water still. I threw her bonnet after her.

Well, that's how it was. I returned to the house. Eventually there was a hue and cry. Eventually she was found. By the time the search party had trampled the path there was a plethora of footprints. And fortunately the marks where she had struck my cheek were hidden by my beard.

It was not quite possible to hold a double funeral; and I saw to it that they lay in different parts of the churchyard. No one else should lie down with what I had thought to be my Sybil. I saw to it that, unlike Juno's swans, they should not any longer be coupled and inseparable.

Ah, there's the dinner bell. This narrative is nicely timed. It has done me good to write it – confession is good for the soul, they say, but I have been more concerned to lay the facts on paper as a study of the singularly odd delusions that can ensnare the human heart. I must, as Sybil said, have been mad.

I am not mad now. I am extremely in possession of myself and ever shall be. I shall make my way to the stern of the vessel, drop this narrative page by page into its creaming wake, then go below to the Saloon and have my dinner. The first night out to sea one does not dress.

Madame Mantis

Hard to believe now, when so many tanks, so much blood have crushed its colour into a stoic grey, that before the war Budapest was one of the most elegant capitals in Europe. Boulevards, boutiques, tzigane music swooping over the café tables, it was a dazzling place.

To Marjorie's stolid English mind, used to the civil mistrust of social intercourse at home, the charm and the unbounded hospitality of its inhabitants were all slightly larger than life. If you knew one Hungarian, you knew fifty. You were swept dizzily from one family to the next, until twenty-four hours were too few in which to visit all the friends of the friends of your friends, and where one Laszlo or Ilona stood, there now stood dozens, and all of them charming and handsome.

Like its citizens, Budapest was chic and gay and beautifully over-coloured, like characters in the Chauve-Souris. Probably, she thought, it is the snow that makes me think of the Chauve-Souris, with the sun shining on the domes of the Parliament House and the brilliant blue sky and the coloured stones of St Stephen's Church high up on the bastions, all like a Christmas card. And as for Mr Hunjady no non Magyar young man could really be as lean, as brilliant, as charming as he, nor could he really be so eager that an English girl whom he had met only ten minutes ago should come to his mother's tea party.

But of course she went, for Mr Hunjady really did wish it, and besides, Stefan, who was looking after Marjorie while she was in Budapest, was one of his oldest friends.

'The most brilliant mother and son in Europe,' Stefan declared, driving his overpowered car through the snowy streets

73

with the élan of a cavalry charge. 'One day when you have four children and live in Tunbridge Wells you will read of the great Miklas Hunjady and spare for me a little kindness because I introduced you. Miklas is a revolution. He will be the greatest surgeon in the world. You will see. And all – all he owed to his wonderful mother.'

Marjorie had found that without a certain amount of mental reservation she could not live in Budapest without getting dizzy. Even so, she had to admit to herself that there really was something rather remarkable about the Hunjadys, mother and son. A kind of glitter hung about them, as though they were both dusted over with powdered diamonds. The glancing dazzle of their charm hypnotised you like a spinning light.

And what Stefan had said about Miklas really was true. At thirty-two he was already heralded as the next genius of surgery. It was already said that under his fingers madness was plucked out of a brain like the eye from a potato. It is quite impossible, thought Marjorie helplessly, sipping Tokay from a tiny glass in Mrs Hunjady's exquisite drawing-room, it is quite impossible that anyone but a Hungarian could be a genius, young, handsome in that elegant, lean, small-featured Hungarian way, unmarried, charming and devoted to his mother all at the same time. To the Anglo-Saxon mind it was all too perfect to be real. And so was Mrs Hunjady.

She was a small, exquisite, vivacious woman with superbly coiffed silver hair and a complexion like valuable porcelain. She darted, she was still, she chattered, she was silent with the fragile swiftness of a humming-bird. She was witty, she was tender, she was chic; she dominated the room by the magic of her charm; and every now and again her huge and glowing eyes rested on her son.

She might, thought Marjorie without conviction, be French. But no, she could be nothing but Hungarian. There was a wildness buried in the core of the woman which never came from France; it illumined her gay enamelled face and gave her tiny body, in spite of its sixty odd years, its dazzling vitality.

She was adorable to Marjorie. Instead of asking, as most

74

Hungarians did, whether Budapest was not the loveliest city in the world, she declared that only in England could she find repose. 'Your tranquillity, the gentle grass, and all those sweet docile cows in the fields,' she said softly. 'We have a saying here in Hungary, my dear, "Sleep is best on a mother's breast," and to me always England is the mother.' And Marjorie, who lived in Worcestershire, felt her cautious consciousness drifting into Mrs Hunjady's keeping as though under an anaesthetic.

'Well,' said Stefan, as they drove away, 'confess now that for once I have not exaggerated. And it is not only what they are, but what they have been which makes them so astonishing. For their history is an epic.'

Driving more dashingly than ever, because now the snow was swirling in the muted dusk, he told her . . .

In 1906 Mr Hunjady, who was a doctor with enough money to travel where he pleased for the study of medicine rather than be content with what walked in through his consulting-room door, decided to leave the South Americas, where he and his young wife had been for a year or two, and journey home to Hungary via the South Seas and India for the birth of their child. It was not a route which most women would have chosen in the circumstances, but Gitta Hunjady was strong and high-willed, with a little Slav blood in her veins to add wildness to her Magyar courage, and she was not in the least dismayed by the long journey ahead of her. It would give her son spirit, she said – for she knew it would be a son. Her whole soul was set on it, as with some women it is, as though they can fulfil themselves only through their sons.

They sailed from Valparaiso on a bright brisk day in June, and for ten days or so the ship, carrying three other passengers, went well. Then a calm fell, a humid and tensing calm which turned the sea to slowly heaving oil, and then came the hurricane. The ship ran like a frightened hen, half crushed between leaden sky and leaden sea, and in the frenzy and fearfulness of the grip of God it lost its course and struck on a maze of reefs. There were only two boats, and the Hunjadys, one of the passengers and too many of the crew got into one and pulled away in time to see the ship

75

break to pieces, taking the other boat and its passengers with it.

The Hunjady's boat was too heavily laden, and when two of the crew began to quarrel on this account they were without ceremony pushed into the sea. Those who were left had little knowledge of navigation, no idea of where they were, and food to last a week, with husbanding.

For five days the boat drifted. One of the crew, injured in the wreck, died and was put overboard. Once, when they caught a glimpse of a ship far off on the horizon, two of the others jumped into the sea to swim madly after it, and were drowned. And at last, using Mrs Hunjady's petticoat for a sail, the boat with its four survivors managed to make a tiny sandy island.

The stores were nearly gone, and there was nothing to eat on the island but a few berries which made them sick and what fish they could manage to snare. There was no fire and no shade, save under the grizzled bushes, and the sun beat down like brass. Fortunately there was a small and unpleasant trickle of fresh water on the island, otherwise they would all have died at once. As it was they were all terribly weak, and Mr Hunjady, a small and delicate man, could hardly stand.

They decided to divide what was left of the food, repair the boat as best they could, and the two members of the crew set off to try and find land, from where they would have help sent to the Hunjadys.

But the boat never reached land, its two occupants were never heard of again. And day after day the Hunjadys on their spit of barren sand eked out the food until there was none left. Then for six days they lived on the chewed roots of the bushes, on leaves, on tiny insects. After that, there was nothing left at all.

Many days later a ship cruising for trade among the little-known islands chanced to see the tattered signal flapping in the hot wind. The boat which reached the island found a wild-eyed, wild-haired woman, thin as a twig save for the swelling which she hid beneath her crossed arms as though to protect it even from death, silent, savage, unbroken. Her husband was dead, drowned, she said trying to catch fish on the far edge of the reef, too weak to save himself.

They brought her back, and tenaciously, fiercely, she brought her child back, too. The will for her child to live had been too strong even for death. Suffering and horror had not weakened her, but had thrust her back to some primitive, animal resistance.

'The miracle of how she alone survived where all the men had died is an eternal mystery,' declared Stefan dramatically. 'It is all in the past. She never speaks of it. You see her now, gay, charming, sophisticated, as though it never was. But believe me, she is still steel and fire underneath where Miklas is concerned. There is nothing she would not do for him. She fought death for him once, and she would do it again.'

Dumbly, Marjorie nodded. Such a story could be true only about Hungarians.

She saw a good deal of Mrs Hunjady in the next few weeks. Miklas, charming as ever, showed no signs of making love to her, and probably for this reason Mrs Hunjady made Marjorie a confidante. Soon Marjorie knew all the passionate struggles and hopes for her son which Mrs Hunjady had made or was prepared to make, all the hungry and relentless love which had preserved and fashioned him, had focused and nourished his genius. For he was a genius, admitted Marjorie, her mind in chaos from the dazzling intimacy of Mrs Hunjady's friendship. He justified whatever battles had been fought for him.

On Christmas Eve the Hunjadys gave a dinner party. The elegant house, with its huge stoves and its double windows shut against the ice-breath from the plains, was stuffed with lovely painted women and tall elegant men, and the snug air purred with soft Hungarian words. The Hunjadys moved among the guests, like sparks of light struck from a diamond, and for Marjorie the rich food, the wine, the polyglot gaiety merged and misted into complete unreality.

Conversation rode in on waves of laughter, compliments bloomed everywhere like charming, ephemeral flowers. She heard the man between herself and Mrs Hunjady declare that it was impossible so small a hand should be strong enough to bear so impressive a signet ring, and saw Mrs Hunjady stretch out her tiny hand with the pointed painted nails and the ring upon it, laughing her brittle musical laughter.

'You like it? It is very dear to us Hunjadys. It is worn always by the head of the house, and must not be taken off till we are lying in our coffin. When I die, it will be taken from my finger by Miklas and worn by him until he dies. That is an old family rule, never broken for many hundreds of years. Yes, it was my husband's ring.'

Tinselly, unreal, the evening swept on and away. And it wasn't until she was on the point of falling asleep that night that Marjorie gave a little gasp. For if Mr Hunjady was drowned off the edge of a reef, how did his ring come to be on Mrs Hunjady's finger?

And with a little sick lump of coldness in her vitals, she remembered that Mrs Hunjady never ate meat.

*

Lines of communication

*

There are many such men, you understand. Unfortunately for us women. And they always marry. It becomes necessary, therefore, for a woman with sense to consider very carefully before she commits herself. One learns caution. I've no doubt women have learned caution from men like that all over the world, in New York and London and Timbuctoo.

This specimen was in Paris – still is, come to that. His name was Aristide Monnet, and he and his wife had the apartment next to mine when I knew them. At least, it was one apartment really, cut in half, you understand, three rooms for them, two for me. We didn't meet much, not me and him. But the walls were thin, hein, and he wasn't one to keep his voice down when he did happen to speak. It was modest, this apartment, for the franc isn't what it used to be and one must live as best one can. Up the hill towards Sacré Coeur, it was – one of those tall grey houses with shabby shutters, and the only breath of air you get in the hot weather is if you take a chair out on to the pavement like everyone else.

But convenient, for my work and his. He was a waiter, worked in one of those arty restaurants on top of the hill, where they serve champagne to English tourists and smother the walls with local daubs. Les Cloîtres Gastronomique, they called it. Gave you a dirty look if you ordered vin ordinaire, but it was well worth drinking. Oh yes, I've been taken there sometimes, one gets around . . .

This Monsieur Aristide was a big dark chap with a moustache, about forty, I suppose, and nothing particular to look at. It beats me, the men that get married. Some women will tie themselves to anything just to be called Madame. Me, I'd rather be self-supporting. Mind you, there was nothing actually wrong with Aristide, he was just glum. A great dark glum type that sent your spirits down just to look at him. And silent – if you got six words from him you were lucky.

She was different, Hortense. We got friendly after a bit. He was out from noon to midnight mostly, and she and I got into the habit of having a bit of a talk in the afternoons when I'd got myself dressed and had something to eat. The things she'd tell me – well, not that exactly, it was more the things she hadn't got to tell me.

She was small and thin, a few years younger than him, and nothing to look at. But you could see, if she'd only taken some trouble with herself, she'd not be half bad. With make-up and her hair done properly and a bit of gaiety to fill her out, she'd pass easily. As it was, there was nothing of her. Just a drab, sad little housewife with no one to talk to. That was where I came in. I heard it all, though it was little enough.

They'd been married nine years, and he'd always been a waiter. They had a week's honeymoon at Boulogne, and every day since then, more or less, she'd been on her own from noon to midnight. On his days off he went and fished in the Seine. They hadn't any kids. She always used to cry when we got to that bit. 'He says a child would disturb his rest,' she'd say, 'and of course its true, it would. You see, he works so hard, he must have his sleep out in the mornings. And at night too, when he comes back. It wouldn't do at all, naturally,' and she'd start crying like anything.

I'd heard him coming back – Mon Dieu, it was one of the causes why we weren't on good terms. Mostly it didn't matter, for naturally I myself am usually out late. But when I return I inconvenience no one, I realise there are others who are fast asleep. But Monsieur Aristide was a different matter. Thump thump up the stairs, scratch scratch at the keyhole, bang of the door. Thump thump into the kitchen, and then 'Hortense!' 'Ah yes, Aristide' and I'd hear the bedsprings creak as she jumped out and put on her dressing-gown and went scampering out to make him his supper. He couldn't make it himself and she couldn't leave it ready for him. 'He's so tired, you see,' she'd say to me,

80

'And it wouldn't be right to let him come home and wait on himself after waiting on other people all day.' When they were first married she'd started cooking for him then as a kind of a joke, putting on an apron, cloth over her arm, pretending to show him the menu. 'Oh, he used to laugh then,' she'd say, 'He used to give me a kiss and call me . . .' she slid me a shy look, 'call me his maîtresse d'hotel. But I don't know. Somehow the years have eaten up all that foolishness.' And she'd sigh, and smile a little, and you could see she still thought tenderly of that bridegroom who'd disappeared.

One must be fair. Me, I'm not a fool, and although I couldn't stand him, one must be fair. He wasn't a cruel type, he didn't mean to be anything but a good husband. It was just that, like so many men, he had lost the habit of communication. He had made his effort, captured his Hortense, and thereafter ceased to exert himself. His wife and his slippers – very much the same thing by now. He did not communicate his thoughts to his slippers, nor expect them to converse with him. It happens very often with selfish men. A woman has need of caution when the proposal is made, she should consider it calmly and try to see whether the shutter will come down between her soul and that of the man who now, eh bien, has such a passionate eloquence! Oh yes, there's a great deal to be said for frequently changing one's coat.

Now one day something happened to these two, and you must take my word for it that this is how it was. Some I heard and some I supposed, and I'm a practical woman not given to fantasies, hein?

One night our Monsieur Aristide comes home from Les Cloîtres Gastronomique, thump thump thump up the stairs. He enters the apartment, he advances to the kitchen, he calls for his wife. As usual, she answers him, scrambles out of bed, and hastens to wait upon him. He is bent over on a chair removing his boots, for his feet hurt him, and he has long given up troubling even to look at his wife, let alone greet her in any way that would gladden a woman's heart. He removes his boots, he massages his toes, he reaches for his slippers under the table and inserts his

81

tired feet. He leans back in his chair, takes his paper from his pocket, reaches out for the glass of wine his wife has placed for him, and reads.

Then, dimly, something warns him all is not as it should be. An uneasiness steals over the back of his neck. He cannot concentrate. He looks up. His wife is busy at the stove as usual, her back towards him, as usual. But it is a different back. It is a back clad not, as is usual, in a dressing-gown of plum-coloured wool, shapeless, shabby, and of a hue so repulsive that one wonders that it was ever created, but a back of peach-coloured satin, worn, it is true, but perfectly cut to cling where it should cling and drape where it should drape, and surmounted on neck and bosom by trembling fronds of peach-coloured marabout.

For a moment he stares, unable to believe his eyes. But he says nothing. That is not his way. No, he stares, and then he turns his eyes to the clock ticking away on the cupboard-top. All is well. He has returned no earlier than usual, it is something past midnight. The peach-coloured hips quiver as Madame stirs vigorously a savoury saucepan. She is oblivious of him. He stares again, and over his heavy face with the moustache so, a look comes, at once wary and incredulous. He gets to his feet and, still without a word, goes – a little quickly, I think – into the bedroom. It appears to be empty, as usual, but our friend nevertheless examines the cupboards and peers under the bed. He even tries the handle of the door which separates my rooms from theirs, but it is, naturally, locked. All is as it should be. He returns, reseats himself and, with an effort, takes up once more his newspaper. Over it, and over his food when he thinks she is not looking, he watches her. But he says nothing. And she says nothing either, because she has learned not to.

Next day, before he leaves for work and while she is out marketing, he searches the drawers of her meagre dressing table and turns her second handbag inside out. I know, because he leaves the door open and I happen to pass by and see him at it. He finds nothing, for his expression is baffled. That night he wakes no one by thumping up the stairs, but creeps up as softly as a cat and throws open the bedroom door. Hortense sits up with a scream.

'Aristide! It's you. Mon Dieu, what's happened?'

'Nothing.'

'You look so strange. Are you ill? Great heavens, it's only half past eleven!'

'Give me my supper.'

'Of course.'

The bedsprings creak, there's a rustle as she draws on the dressing-gown. As she passes him he seizes her by the arm. She cries out. 'Aristide! What is it? You're hurting me!' He releases her, and whimpering a little, she prepares his meal.

But he still says nothing.

Thenceforward jealousy holds Aristide Monnet in its profound grip. He goes to work as late as possible, he comes home as early as he can. In the slack afternoon hours he darts home down the hill to see what his wife is doing. He gives up fishing. And every few days he searches diligently her personal belongings. His mind, usually so dead, is alive, is pulsing with a terrible conundrum! Why does his wife suddenly display herself in an alluring peach-coloured dressing gown? His eyes, usually so dull, are now alight with passion. His movements, usually so slow, are forceful. He is not a changed man. He is the same man, liberated from himself by torment.

Hortense is quite bewildered. Her little confidences come to me in fits and starts. 'He follows me about,' she said, and a look foolish but infinitely tender illumines a face already a little more rosy. 'His eyes seldom leave me. When he goes to work – he kisses me passionately. And when he comes home . . .'

'But he says nothing?' I asked.

'Oh no, he says nothing at all. But I feel he has something on his mind,' she said. Then she sighed, but not with melancholy. 'If only he would say something, really it would be almost like the old days when we were first married.'

Now it so happened that I had at this time a friend – I wouldn't intrude my own affairs here, you understand, but that it's

83

necessary in the tale of the Monnets. This friend – he called himself Toto – was – how shall I put it? – something of a rascal. Clever, young, with a finger in many pies, not altogether an honest type, not altogether agreeable, and yet, it's hard to explain, he had a way with him. Me, I'm a practical woman, and I can see two crows in a snowfield as well as anyone. But there was something about Toto, I must admit – besides, he was ravishingly handsome.

One evening, at a time when normally our Monsieur Aristide was hardly yet counting up the many and extravagant tips the English tourists had been intimidated into leaving him, I was startled by a terrible commotion. Sudden shouts, groans and curses reverberated on the stairs. The front door of the apartment burst open with a violence unimaginable, and crashing headlong to the floor the terrified Hortense and I, each drawn to our respective doors, beheld a whirling, threshing mass of masculine rage. On top, heaving and battering, we recognised Aristide himself, his face contorted with fury, and from his lips coming a stream of language such as to command respect. Beneath, wriggling like a snake and with his beautiful hair disordered over a bloody nose, was – hélas! – poor Toto. He, too, was uttering a formidable vocabulary, but as Aristide was alternately banging his head upon the floor and throttling him, not much could be distinguished.

With a scream Hortense threw herself upon them, crying: 'Assassin! Help, help! Police! Assassin!', trying to disentangle Aristide and at the same time slap poor Toto's face. She was wearing the peach-coloured dressing-gown, and as it was a danger both to itself and her in the present mêlée, I intervened with a shrewd kick in Monsieur Aristide's ribs. With a groan he rolled sideways into her arms, and I was able to release poor Toto. He looked so droll, I couldn't help laughing. He had bloodied his nose by crashing through the front door with Aristide on his back, cut his mouth on the floorboards, and now had a black eye where, one supposes, Hortense had caught him. He even, unhappily, was spitting out a tooth, and his suit – an affair very Yankee, very 'zoot' – was in a state beyond description.

'Pig, robber, son of a something something!' Aristide was shouting.

'Assassin! Thief! Aristide, my hero, my lion!' Hortense accompanied him shrilly.

'And you, you something something!' Aristide turned on her. 'At least I've ruined his looks for you now, hein? He's not so handsome now, eh, your pretty little monsieur, your . . .'

But there, there's no necessity to labour the situation further.

Toto, as soon as he could walk, borrowed five hundred francs from me towards a new suit, and disappeared for ever. Ah well, these things happen, there's no need to weep over them. And after the things Monsieur Aristide said to me about my friends and various other affairs before that night was out, and I'd told him a few particulars I'd had on my mind since I first moved in there, well, naturally, I packed my things and moved out the next day, and I've never seen him since.

I've seen her, though – and the baby. A dear little thing, but slow to talk. Hortense – well, such happiness makes you want to weep or laugh, you don't know which. She says Monsieur Aristide spends all his days off with her, and always gets home early. And sometimes, she says proudly, he has queer moods of searching her belongings.

But he's never said anything. Not even when her own monstrosity came back from the cleaners and she returned to me the peach-coloured dressing gown.

Ah well, there are many such men in the world, you understand – and not incapable of happiness.

The funny side

*

As had been his custom for the thirty odd years he had been in business, Mr Frederick Peebles bought an evening newspaper at Waterloo.

And after successfully battling for a seat he settled down with more than usual satisfaction to digest the day's happenings; for not only was it a dank and nasty November night, not only was he weary after his day's work, not only was there a full report of Manchester City v Yorkshire Wanderers, but there was also a double column account on page one of the latest, and as yet unsolved, murder. And Mr Peebles, mild-mannered, shining-pated little ledger clerk of St Mary Axe, loved a good murder.

Wedged against his neighbour in the swaying, smoky-lit carriage Mr Peebles began to read:

'New developments in the Burton Park Estate murder are expected, which, it is hoped, will lead to the identification of the woman whose savagely battered body was discovered on a lonely piece of waste ground on the Burton Park Estate on Wednesday. So far all efforts to establish the victim's identity have failed.'

Mr Peebles laid down the paper for a moment in order to light his pipe. His neighbour glanced at him, and remarked chattily: 'Shocking thing, this murder.'

'Shocking!' said Mr Peebles.

''Pon my soul, you can't call your life your own these days,' continued his neighbour.

'That's right,' said Mr Peebles, 'And the police seem absolutely useless.'

It was the neighbour's turn to nod his head. 'That's right. Don't know what they're coming to these days. Shocking, that's what it is.'

'That's right,' said Mr Peebles; and after a short ruminative pause both gentlemen resumed their reading.

At first sight the murder seemed simple enough. A middle-aged woman dead in the bushes, the weapon – an iron bar from a nearby building plot – lying beside her, a quantity of footprints . . . Nothing very perplexing here. Yet no one knew the woman. Dozens of people, fearful yet thrilled, had failed to identify her. No one had heard or seen anything unusual that night in Burton Park, and besides, it had been foggy.

'It is hoped that once the identity of the victim is established the police will be able to pursue their enquiries with greater facility. At the moment they are hampered by lack of any clue to the victim's life or associates which might suggest a motive for the murder.'

Murder . . .

Mr Peebles looked out at the flying lights of the suburban High Streets.

Yes, he had always been interested in murder. And particularly so in this one, as he happened to have committed it himself.

It had been ridiculously simple, really. After the first shock of opening the door and finding Maisie outside he'd been very level-headed about the whole business. Ah well, he was always telling little Fred that the secret of success was a calm head. 'Never get flustered, my boy. Never lose your head. That's the way to get on in this life.' Quite right, too.

Of course, luck had been on his side. First of all Dora and Freddie being out, and then the fog, and then that iron bar lying handy . . .

He'd been sitting quietly at home last Wednesday evening, listening to the wireless. Dora had taken Freddie to the doctor's to have a whitlow lanced, poor little chap. Brave, he'd been, too. And then there'd been a knock at the door and when he opened it, there was Maisie.

He knew her at once, although it was fourteen years or more since he saw her last.

'Hullo,' she said, quite cheerfully.

He stood in his slippers and shirtsleeves, holding the door, gaping at her.

'Well, I won't wait to be asked in,' she said, and walked past him into the hall.

'You can't come in here,' he said, and caught her arm.

'Rubbish, dear,' she answered. 'This is my house and you're my husband.'

It was quite true. She'd gone off one day fourteen years ago and never come back – just left a note: 'Dear Fred, I've had enough. You needn't ask me to come back because my mind's made up. Please send my things to Charing Cross station Left Luggage where perhaps I will pick them up. The money for the laundry is on the kitchen mantelpiece. Love, Maisie.'

That was the last he'd heard of her. For two years he had lived as a bachelor, and quite enjoyed it too at first. It made a change, after Maisie. Then he met Dora. For a long time he hesitated, then finally his loneliness and his longing for her became too intense to be borne. He married her, banking on Maisie never turning up again.

He'd been a fool actually to marry Dora, he saw that now. But it was one chance in a hundred Maisie finding him after all this time. And now here she was, in his kitchen and Dora only gone out for half an hour.

'You've got to clear out,' he said.

'Where to?'

'Where you came from.'

She laughed. She had grown stout and placid. 'My wandering days are over,' she said. 'I've come home, Fred.'

'But you can't. I've married again.'

She stared at him for a moment. 'Well, you are a juggins. That's bigamy, Fred.'

'I know it,' he answered irritably. Just like Maisie to make him out a fool before she'd been back five minutes. He put on his coat.

'Look, we can't talk here. Dora and the boy'll be back any minute. We've got to talk this over, I see that. I'll treat you fair. Only we can't stay here.'

She had seen his point of view, and although it was a nasty night she agreed to go out and talk it over.

And as they walked along the foggy, half-built roads towards the outskirts of the Estate, she told him again that she'd come home. She was quite firm about it. She was getting on in years, she said, and perhaps she ought never to have left him. It was a pity about Dora and the boy – but after all, she had first call on him, and besides, she hadn't any money.

'Let bygones be bygones, Fred,' she said, and laid her hand on his arm quite affectionately. He couldn't make her see that he didn't want her back, that he was happy with Dora and little Fred. She just went on talking fondly at him, ignoring everything but her own purpose. 'And after all,' she said, 'look at it from my side. I've got to live.'

And swiftly the retort had come to him: Why?

The train drew into the station, and Mr Peebles rose.

'Well, good night,' he said to his neighbour.

'Good night. Hope they'll have caught him by tomorrow.'

'That's right,' said Mr Peebles, and got out.

It was two days before the papers reported that Maisie had been identified, and then only by a boarding-house keeper with whom she'd lodged for one night. She had told the woman that she'd just arrived in England from New Zealand, which was true; but for some reason of her own she had called herself Mrs Fletcher. There were no photographs of her for the newspapers to publish, and anyway she wouldn't have many friends left in England now to recognise her. As far as the public was concerned she was just a middle-aged woman whom nobody knew or missed.

Sad, really, thought Mr Peebles.

He read the newspapers every day with great interest. It never occurred to him that he might be caught. He'd had a few nasty moments the first day or so when the papers kept on saying 'an arrest is imminent'; but he knew now that was just to save their faces. They didn't know a thing, really.

And in spite of a very natural bias in his own favour, he couldn't help thinking that it was a scandalous thing. The police ought to be able to find out who did it. They ought to be able to find out who Maisie really was. Once they did that, they could begin looking for a motive. Of course, Mr Peebles appreciated that bigamy was a very pretty motive, pointing straight to himself. But even so, putting aside the personal aspect of it, they really ought to be able to do better than they had.

'It's the system,' he declared over the supper table to Dora, 'The system's all wrong. They don't go about it the right way.'

'It must be ever so difficult,' said Dora.

'Of course it's difficult. Murderers are men with brains, my dear. They don't want to be caught any more than I do. But it's the police's job to be smarter than they are, see? That's what we pay them for.'

And day by day Mr Peebles began to feel not only contempt but indignation at the failure of the police. From what he read in the newspapers they let real clues slip through their fingers, they rushed off after things which had no connection with Maisie at all. Mr Peebles fairly danced with impatience sometimes when he read such statements as: 'The police are anxious to interview a man who is known to have travelled from South Burton to Tooting on the night of the murder.' Good heavens, he had been nowhere near Tooting then or since!

Or: 'Evidence regarding sounds of a quarrel heard on November 20 near the south side of the Estate is regarded as of importance by the police.' There had been no quarrel. Maisie never knew a thing.

The days grew into weeks. Mr Peebles' contempt grew into open derision. Obsessed, he talked on the subject with eloquence and passion to anyone who would listen. So much passion that he had words with Mr Glossop, the head clerk.

'The police are a very fine body of men,' Mr Glossop said majestically, 'and I wouldn't put it upon myself to cast aspersions on their way of working. Have you considered the difficulties with which they have to contend? The thousands of clues, statements, misguided help, not to mention the abuse from persons like yourself, Mr Peebles. If I were you, I think I should save my criticism for subjects you know something about,' and he passed on, smirking.

Insufferable old ass, fumed Mr Peebles over his ledger. Pompous old jackass! He and his police – thought he and they knew everything! Well, he was wrong, see? Mr Peebles knew a thing or two. Old ass! Ticking him off in front of the juniors, too. He'd like to make old Glossop take back what he'd said – make him apologise, make him acknowledge he was wrong.

But although Mr Peebles couldn't do that, he did get level with Mr Glossop, for he followed him home an evening or so later, and hit him on the back of his fat head with a paper-weight tied up in a handkerchief.

It was all over the papers next morning: CITY MAN FOUND DYING IN ROAD – HANDKERCHIEF CLUE. Mr Glossop died without regaining consciousness, and the police had a second murder to solve.

'And can they do it? No!' cried Mr Peebles in the 'Walrus Arms' that evening. 'Why? Because the system's all wrong. A man's bashed on the head outside his house one evening, and the police can't even find out why. They've got a clue! They've got a handkerchief!'

'It's got no marks on it or anything,' said someone. 'It's just a plain white handkerchief like you or me might have.'

'But it's something!' insisted Mr Peebles, his bald head

glistening with impatience. 'Of course the man who did it's not a fool! But if he'd left his name and address on it they couldn't catch him.'

He wrote to the papers. He said it was a scandal that the taxpayers who paid for protection couldn't get it. He wrote so often, they gave up acknowledging them.

And still day after day he read such things as: 'The police attach importance to the statement of an errand boy who saw a suspicious-looking man waiting in a black saloon car near Willoughby Road on the night of the murder.'

'Wild goose chase!' snorted Mr Peebles. 'Wasting our money. It's a disgrace!'

As for poor Maisie, they seemed to have given her up as a bad job.

It was when a woman stated she had passed a man who seemed to be following Mr Glossop (and she was quite right, Mr Peebles remembered her) and the next day a complete stranger came forward, said he was the man, was identified by the woman, and very properly dismissed as having nothing to do with the crime, that Mr Peebles began to see the funny side.

For there was, he saw, no end to the follies of his fellow men. There was always someone to swear they heard a scream or saw a man or were passing by at the time. And the beauty of it was that although Mr Peebles knew these claims to be fantastic, the public believed them all, and each one was investigated with meticulous thoroughness.

Life suddenly became rich for Mr Peebles. Maisie was gone, Mr Glossop was gone, and the man who succeeded him was a very decent chap. He had Dora and little Fred and his job and, best of all, his huge and secret, splendid joke. All over England the police were wracking their brains to find *him*, Frederick Peebles of Burton Park. The Big Five spent all their time driving from one end of England to the other after supposed clues. Every newspaper was hungry for an arrest. And here he was all the time, doing his work, being good to Dora, educating his son, with the power to play such pranks on the police – and the public too, and the newspapers – as would keep them sleepless for years to come.

In a fit of mischief one day he even wrote a letter to Scotland Yard. 'The Police are fools,' it said. 'Their system is wrong. Why don't they look nearer home and save the taxpayers' money? I could tell them a thing or two because I did them both.' He didn't even bother to disguise his writing very much, although he posted it from the City to make it a little difficult.

Dora couldn't make him out these days, he was always chuckling to himself.

But when, weeks afterwards, he read the following statement, he felt that humour could go no further: 'After intensive enquiries, during which time Scotland Yard's ace crime sleuths have investigated something like a thousand clues and voluntary statements, it is understood that the police know the identity of the murderers of both Mrs Maisie Fletcher, whose body was found ... and of Alfred Bradbury Glossop, who died from injuries ... They are waiting until their cases are complete before making arrests.'

Mr Peebles guffawed. 'Here, Dora,' he cried, 'look at this.'

Dora looked. 'I don't see what's so funny,' she said.

He slapped his knee hilariously. 'They think they know who it is!' he cried. 'But that's all bluff, my dear, bluff! They're no wiser than what you are. And never will be!'

'Do stop it, Fred,' said Dora fretfully. 'You act so queer these days, I don't know what's got into you,' and she went back into the kitchen to finish the ironing.

The beauty of Mr Peebles' joke grew and grew until he felt it would burst through his head and set the whole world laughing. And coming home one night just before Christmas he knew that he must – he simply must – play another trick, must experience again the exquisite humour of duping the world.

He could hardly wait to get out of the train. He pushed past the ticket collector like a madman, shaking with laughter. He ran in little stops and starts down the cold streets homewards. He would use his own poker this time. Or, better still, Dora's own iron. Then she would see – then she would appreciate the deliciousness of his jest. It was time he let her share it with him – and how she would laugh, how she would admire his beautiful hoax on everyone. Even though Dora would be dead, she would know, she would see the funny side of it and laugh and laugh with him . . .

He shook so much with laughing that he could hardly fit his key into the lock.

He need not have troubled, for two plainclothes policemen opened the front door to him.

*

Tenants

*

I have to tell someone. But who? They'd think I was mad. Or Nicky . . . I'm frightened, frightened. And I'm not that kind of person at all really. People always say I'm so capable, so level-headed. And I am. That's why now . . . So if I write it all down perhaps I'll be able to see that it's all imagination, that it's not really . . .

Nicky and I started a thing together about two years ago. I was living with two girls and he was in some sort of a grotty commune thing, so it wasn't all that easy for us to be together. I simply can't do private things in semi-public – people in the next room or due back in half an hour. Nor could Nicky really, although he pretends he could. The thing is, we've both been brought up 'proper'. And although he really has broken away (he left Marlborough before taking his A levels and then he dropped out of LSE because he had this fantastic offer to help start up a sort of pop art magazine, but it only came out once) I honestly haven't. I left home and got a job, of course, and went through various phases, but underneath it all I really like to be tidy and organised, and I daresay that's why I got such a good job that really interests me and pays a bomb.

And really, actually, I'd like to be married. I know it's silly and no one does now unless they're having a baby or something, but I can't help it. I've been conditioned and I just should awfully like to be Nicky's legal, lawful wife. Of course I've never said so, absolutely never so much as hinted. But I suppose maybe he might have sussed.

Because I really do love him. It's not just that I think he's beautiful – he's sort of fine-boned and ethereal, as though his skin was transparent somehow, although he's as strong as a horse – but I love even his faults. He's terribly moody and highly strung, especially when his work's not going right. Then he just goes into a silence. Absolutely withdrawn. It's horrible but I do love him and I have to try and help him sort of come back to me. Usually I can – could.

So to go back to what I was saying first, I decided – we decided we had to find a place together on our own. The idea didn't grab him at first, but after we'd talked it over a bit he said Great.

Well. I looked and looked and honestly, you wouldn't believe the grotty places people think people will pay them to live in. Basements you could grow mushrooms in, attics the rain came into, crumby bits of furniture, filthy old gas stoves. I looked and looked and if there was ever anything halfway decent it had gone before I got there. I began to get really frantic. You know how it is if you finally decide you want to do something, you simply get frantic if you can't do it at once. Nicky said give it a rest, we'd look again later, but I really did want to be with him on our own. Besides, he hadn't been well – bronchitis or something, and he was looking more and more as though made of glass. I longed to take care of him and fatten him up a bit and cosset him and – well, just love him. I do love him.

Then I found it. It was the first floor of one of those terribly ugly Victorian semis in north London, yellowy brick and a portico, laurels in front with dustbins, a straggly garden at the back. Two decent rooms and a bath with a cover over it in the kitchen, and a few bits of not too grotty furniture. The road was dreary but opposite they'd built a new school, all glass and flat roofs and lollipop ladies, so we could see the sky instead of just other ugly houses. Somehow I'd managed to be there first and I had to decide at once, so I did. I took it and paid six months in advance and we moved in the next week.

Nick was funny about it. He prowled around like a cat, sort of sniffing the atmosphere. 'It's got a funny feel to it,' he said, 'sort of – I don't know, echoes.'

'Vibes?' I said, sort of pulling his leg.

'Yes, – maybe. It's sort of – cold.'

'Of course it's cold, it's been empty. An empty place is always cold.'

We painted it up a bit and moved in our own bits and pieces. Nick hadn't much but I'd got – or soon bought – quite a bit – some rugs and I made curtains and we had big cushions to sit on, a kitchen table. I'd got a lot of saucepans and china because I like cooking, and Mummy and Daddy gave us a bed – which was jolly nice of them really because I don't expect they really approved, but they never said a word.

Oh, it was heaven! I'd get up early and clean and polish before even Nicky woke up, and think what we'd have to eat. I'd leave him just waking up, with coffee and an apple (that's all he ever wants) and go off to work simply longing to get back. I'd hurry home in the evening with lovely things to cook and jobs to do like cushion covers or shelves or something, and he'd be there. Sometimes he'd be in a mood and I knew he'd not had a good day, but sometimes we simply fell into each other's arms and went to bed then and there and had our meal afterwards. And almost all our nights were full of love – real lovely warm loving connubial love – that's a lovely word, connubial. Solid. Secure. Like my parents.

And he really seemed content. Sort of stretched out and relaxed, as if he liked this way of life after all. It was bliss. For a little while.

He'd always had moods, I knew that. I hoped that with me they'd grow less because he was as happy as I was. But they didn't. After the first week or two they began to come back. You see, I was out all day and he was there on his own and when I got back he was often all pent up and I'd get it all. Sometimes it was just silence. I hated that. He'd just sort of grunt if I said anything, sagged down on the cushions, not reading, just sort of shut away. But sometimes he'd be restless, walking about with a sort of listening look, although he wouldn't listen to *me*. The restlessness was new; before, he'd always been passive, sunk down in his own gloom.

We'd been there about a month when one day he suddenly said, 'I hate this place.'

I was using the blender and couldn't hear properly and shouted, 'What?'

He absolutely yelled back. 'I hate this place. I hate this bloody place!'

I switched it off. 'Nicky – you can't! It's lovely, it's perfect . . .'

'It's a bloody prison. It hedges me in. You've not been alone here all day, listening, wondering . . .'

'Wondering? What about?'

'Everything. What we're doing here, what people did here before. What goes on.'

'Nothing goes on except us. It's ours.'

'Is it?' He gave me a funny look. 'It's yours maybe, not mine. I hate the bloody place.' Then he went silent and wouldn't speak again for a long time.

I thought I knew what it was. You see, in a way he was right, the flat was more mine than his because I earned more money than he did. Well, actually, I earned it all because I had this fantastic job which I really loved and paid a bomb, and Nicky earned nothing at all. He's a writer – that magazine thing was just the beginning, really he was writing two things, a novel about being a student and dropping out and finding yourself, and then this fantastic television series, sort of plays which acted out all the various philosophical concepts in terms of modern economics that he hoped BBC 2 would do, only it was taking ages because it was all so deep, and he didn't know anyone in TV to give him encouragement.

Of course he couldn't possibly have done a job at the same time as all this writing, so naturally I paid everything and that was fine – I mean, what does it matter who pays, it was us, wasn't it, and lots and lots of men live off their women – that sounds horrid, its not like that a bit. I mean, I had the money, I was earning, so what the hell, me or Social Security? I loved him to, I wanted him to.

Only the thing is, although he agreed in theory – well, you can't have parents and schools and upbringing like ours and get rid of it all as easily as that. I mean, look at me and my feeling I'd like to be married. I mean, what difference does it make whether we are or not? I mean, how silly can you get? But I suppose that just as I felt about that, Nicky felt about me being the breadwinner, deep down. I suppose that was it.

We'd got plenty of friends and they'd all loved the flat and said how lucky we were and all that. We'd been there about six weeks and Ben, who I've known for ever, and this friend of Nicky's were there drinking coffee. It was late, after midnight, Nicky never wants to go to bed (not to sleep, anyway) and Dicky never does either. That's his sort of nickname – he's Nicky's oldest friend, like Ben is mine, they were at school together and went to LSE together only Dicky stayed on, and they got called Nicky and Dicky (Derek really) because they were always around together. He's very good-looking, sort of like the blond one in 'Starsky and Hutch', and very masculine, which is jolly odd because I'm absolutely certain he's gay as a bird. I've never dared say this to Nicky, he'd be furious, but Dicky's got that sort of mocking, amusing, light way about him which makes people laugh but is spiteful underneath very often, especially about me. I've never said anything because maybe I've imagined it and Nicky'd be furious. But I've seen the way Dicky looks at him sometimes and the way he looks at me, and he's always calling me 'the little homemaker' or 'our career lady', two things that Nicky absolutely doesn't want.

So we were all there that evening with our mugs of coffee and Ben said something about going home and Dicky said something about 'hard to leave the cosy nest' and then 'You really have done wonders, love, no one would ever know. And it doesn't bother you?'

'What bothers us?' I said.

'Why – what it was.' Then he paused and looked round in a sort of mock concerned way. 'You can't mean you don't know?'

'Know what?' asked Ben.

'Well . . .' Dicky paused again. 'This is where that murder was. A few years back.'

'A murder?' Only Ben spoke.

'Yes, an 'orrible murder. You can't mean you didn't know?' He knew we didn't. 'Feller strangled his wife, then stuffed her in the cupboard – that one, I shouldn't wonder.' He waved a hand. 'He went on living here, going to work every day, then he killed himself. Neighbours found him, police found her. You must remember it, it was the juiciest since poor old Christie – the Denville Road murder.'

Ben had gone scarlet and shouted, 'You bloody oaf, what d'you want to say that for?' but I couldn't say anything and Nicky simply sat there, staring at Dicky with his mouth half open and an awful sort of glazed look on his face.

Well, after that the absolute nightmare began. Actual nightmare for me. I'd struggle awake trying to scream, nothing but mumbles and twitches to help me out of the horror, and when I managed to thresh myself awake I'd find Nicky lying there beside me with his eyes open, wide awake as though he wasn't really there. And in the morning he'd sometimes pretend to be asleep when I left.

We never talked about what Dicky had said. I couldn't. I couldn't even think about it, except that I thought about it all the time I wasn't actually at work. I thought about the fury and terror of the thing itself but more I thought about the days and nights afterwards, when that man was here alone, pretending to the outside world, living with his inside hell, cracking . . .

I shut my mind against it, I busied myself more and more on making the flat our own, bright and clean and new, and I wrapped Nicky round with all the love that was in me to blot out his thoughts too. I thought about moving and looked at advertisements in newspapers and noticeboards – I even went to see one or two without telling Nicky, for I couldn't let him see how upset I was, all my thoughts were on calming him, pretending it hadn't happened, we'd not been told, there was nothing to know. But housing was even more hopeless now than when we'd found the flat. And we'd still got nearly four months paid for. How could we leave? As soon as we could, we would. I'd go on looking. But not say anything to Nicky, not let him know how frightened I was by what Dicky's words had done to him.

He was so silent, much more than before. Or else very gay – the old use of the word. A sort of frantic gaiety that seemed to glitter and flash as though he were made of metal. I guessed he'd been seeing Dicky when he was like that – I don't know what he did when I was at work all day, but he wasn't writing. When I asked him about it, he looked at me oddly and said, 'I can't write now, I'm not that sort of person any more.'

One evening I came back and he was just sitting in the dark. He didn't say Hullo or anything, just sat there looking at me with a peculiar sort of laughter in his face as though he had some private joke which was – I don't know, spiteful somehow.

He watched me a bit and then he said, 'They weren't married, you know. They were just living together – like us.'

'Who?' but I knew.

'Ted Frensham and his girl. Our former tenants.' He grinned. 'She was pregnant.'

I blurted out, 'I'm not pregnant.'

'Great. But she was. I read it all up in the library back files of the newspapers. She was nagging him to get married.'

'I don't want to hear about it.' I made as much noise as I could with the supper pots and pans. He just sat there, grinning.

'He left a note when he killed himself – on the mantelpiece, I expect – there.' He gestured towards ours. 'He said he felt hemmed in. Trapped. I can understand that.'

'I can't. He could have gone away.'

'Perhaps he didn't really want to.' Then he got up and came over to me and put his arms round me, and for a little while he was the Nicky I'd loved for ever.

But that was the last time. Bit by bit it was as though a shadow was growing somewhere – it was at the back of his eyes when he was in one of his silences; and it was somewhere just behind me sometimes, just out of sight – a shadow, a shape, a feeling. I knew it was all imagination. Dicky had done it on purpose, to break up

Nicky and me. He knew how suggestible Nicky was, even if the story hadn't been true. But it was true, and he'd made sure Nicky went and checked up on it. Ted Frensham had murdered his girlfriend in Denville Road seven years ago, how could we not believe that the echoes could still be heard?

'You're a great pair,' said Dicky, 'the stuff the Empire is made of. Horror movie into love nest with a wave of the homemaker's wand. No ghostly tappings or moanings, mysterious squeals in the night. No malign presence – love conquers all.'

'Belt up,' said Ben. He got fearfully uptight about it and tried to shut Dicky up if ever they were there at the same time and Dicky started picking and digging away at it, as he did, always. 'When people are dead they're dead, it's over and done with.'

'You don't believe in ghosts? In "sensitives" that can pick up the violence left behind?'

'No, I bloody don't.'

'Nicky does.' Dicky smiled. 'Nicky's a sensitive. He knows things get left behind when murder's been done . . .'

Ben hit him. Not very hard because they were both sitting down but he cut Dicky's lip. Nicky simply went white and sat there, silent, but Dicky said spitefully, 'There, you see – a presence is still here.'

It's hard to describe the next bit. It wasn't just Nick, but it was me too. The flat wasn't ours any more, it was as though there was always someone else in the next room, keeping quiet, holding their breath, listening. Listening to Nick listening. Some of the time I didn't feel it – I had to be out all day, I made myself busy and cheerful when I got back, we played records and had friends in or went out. But when we were on our own, if we were quiet, then, behind the next room's door, outside in the passage, the listening began again. I'd get up to go into that room or the passage, banging my feet, terrified but determined to face it out. The room was always empty, quite silent. But presently, in a

102

different place, the listening would start again, the shadow grow again.

That's all I ever heard – the listening. But Nick heard and saw more. He didn't tell me but I knew. I could see him begin to draw away from me, just sitting, his eyes alert, flickering as though trying to follow something, trying to hear something. When I tried to get near to him he almost snarled at me. He wouldn't eat the things I bought specially because he liked them. When we made love, which was hardly ever now, he didn't care about me at all, it was just quick and savage as though he hated me. A different Nicky looked out of his eyes and hated me.

At last I said, 'Nick, let's leave. Let's go away for a bit. We can go to a hotel even, I can pay.'

'I'm sure you can,' he said and his face and his voice were horrible. 'You've got me by the short and curlies, big earner, big boss lady. Why not ask Daddy to buy us a nice little semi with room for a pram in the patio? You go if you want to – go on, piss off if you want to.' I began to cry. He just stared at me. 'That's right,' he said, and his voice wasn't a bit like his but rough and with a sort of accent, 'you always cry, don't you, you cow. That's how you got me, isn't it. That's how you bloody tie me down . . .' Then he slammed out of the room.

The listening closed in on me like a fog and through it all there seemed to run a sort of snigger.

I should have gone. But I loved him. How could I leave him on his own in that place with whatever, whoever it was creeping in on him, taking him over, my poor unhappy love? I was stronger than he was, tougher. I suppose he resented it, resented all the things I was and he wasn't, like being successful and earning a lot and being efficient and level-headed and, well yes, conventional, even if not by Daddy and Mummy's standards. But it was more than that now. He was changing. He was Nicky, yes, high-strung and insecure, but he was someone else too, someone ugly and vengeful and bottled up, whose violence lurked in the empty rooms, behind closed doors, under the floors, listening, whispering, reaching out to enter and take possession . . .

103

At work I was promoted. I was given a whole small section of my own. It meant more money, and I went out without telling Nicky and I found us a super bed-sit, kitchen and bath in a modern block of flats with no character and no ghosts, and I mortgaged my pay for a month's rent as from the following week. We would be free again. Ted Frensham couldn't follow us there. Nothing could follow us there, we'd be on our own as we'd been before and Nick would start writing again and love me again and all would be well. We still had two months to run on the flat but I didn't care.

I went home and told Nicky.

He was sitting in the dark as usual – twilight really, because the days were getting longer and the birds were still settling down in the trees outside the window. I took the shopping bag through to the kitchen and came back, taking off my coat. 'So we'll pack up at the weekend and be out of here Sunday. We can use Ben's car, he won't mind going backwards and forwards. We can leave what we haven't room for until we find a really permanent place, and start from there.'

He got very slowly to his feet. 'You bitch,' he said. 'You bossy, arrogant, interfering bitch.' He came towards me. 'D'you think I'm going on poncing off you? D'you think you can tie me up and lug me off like I was a piece of furniture? D'you think I'm going to be tied to you and some squalling filthy little bastard for the rest of my days? I've had enough, d'you hear me, I've had a bloody nough!'

He reached out and he put his hands round my neck and he began to choke me. I couldn't scream and I pulled and pulled at his fingers but they were like wire biting into me, his whole body was trembling as though a current was passing through it and up his arms and into his fingers, pressing and pressing, and his face was sort of swimming above me as my knees gave and I began to fall but was held up by those wiry trembling arms, and his face with the lips drawn back like a dog snarling, a dog intent on a bone, fixed and savage and quite, quite without . . .

The telephone rang. It shocked. For a moment we hung there, he and I, frozen – me on my knees with my hands trying to undo his, he bending over me, wire arms braced to the fingers. A dazed look came over his face and he dropped me. I fell to the floor, choking and sobbing. In a daze he stared at the telephone as it rang and rang. Then he crossed the room and lifted the receiver. A voice squawked in it.

'Yes,' Nick said thickly, 'Yes. You what?' His gaze moved to me and a kind of horror began to thaw the mask that had been his face. 'Gone? I see. Well, thanks . . . Yes, sure, I'll tell her. I'll tell her.'

He put down the receiver though the telephone still squawked, and stood staring at me, his face seeming to break up, disintegrate like something under water.

'That was Ben,' he said. He sat down slowly. 'He checked at the Town Hall. The Frensham house was opposite. Where the school is.'

I had pulled myself to my knees. 'The school . . . ?'

'The Frensham house was pulled down. It's gone. He never lived here.'

I croaked, 'Never lived here? No murder? Nothing . . . ?'

We stared at each other. It was dark by now, but a street lamp shone in. He was a black shape motionless against the window.

He said dully, 'He never lived here. He was never here. There was only us.'

Good investments

*

Eunice Christine Hilda Bradshaw grew up in the crisply stony seaside town of Seaham with her maternal Auntie Florence, her father having been killed on active service in 1944, her mother dying of heart trouble two years later. Eunice was in her late teens by this time, studying clerical skills at the local Polytechnic. She and Auntie Florence knew each other well, as the sisters had lived near to each other, and the transference from one terrace villa to another was painless. Auntie Florence was a dressmaker, a stout exclamatory woman who had never married, and she doted on Eunice – so clever, so competent, such a church-goer, a sweet girl. And it was all true.

Eunice graduated through several jobs, each better than the last; and for the past twenty-seven years she had been head of the department dealing with Bereavement Claims in the Seaham branch of a national charitable organisation.

She was a neat, refined woman now, neither fat nor thin, discreetly made-up (but nothing so vulgar as eye shadow, merely powder, pink lipstick, and on off days perhaps a brush of rouge), with hair parted at the side with a half fringe and which grew just a little browner with each fortnightly visit to the hairdresser. She ran her department impeccably, with a smile and a word of praise when merited. She ran Auntie Florence's house impeccably also, especially as Auntie grew older and fatter and weaker, leaving more and more of it to Eunice and never ceasing to exclaim what a treasure she was. And she was.

She liked everything to be dainty. Frilled curtains, cushions and aprons; flowered bed linen; potted plants in pretty containers standing on doilies; embroidered tray cloths and nightdress cases.

106

She cooked delicious cakes, scones, puddings, even made fudge and fondants. She tried out whimsical recipes from magazines, such as Sponge Easter Bunnies, Chocolate Yule Logs, Guy Fawkes Brandy Snaps. A spot of spillage in the kitchen was whisked away in a trice, the oven was almost as pure as the day it was installed, the teacloths rinsed and drying after each use, and herself and Auntie sitting in front of the television eating dainty snacks off trays daintily laid with embroidered cloths and matching flowered crockery.

'What a girl you are!' Auntie would wheeze, tucking in. 'What a treasure!'

'Silly Auntie!' Eunice would murmur indulgently, 'It's my pleasure.'

And it was.

So when Auntie died Eunice felt it keenly. People were very kind; she had, of course, the support of the church among whose congregation she had many friends. Auntie had left the house to her and a few – a very few – thousand pounds in the bank. Eunice was due to retire the following year, when she would be sixty. The pension would not be much but she had some savings in the Building Society; she would be able to manage.

But she missed Auntie. She missed her wheezing presence, her cries of love and appreciation. She missed having an audience for her excellence; making rock cakes and peppermint creams for the Church Bazaar was not the same, glad though she was to do it, as making them for immediate, face-to-face applause. She missed having someone to demonstrate her virtues to.

She had caused a rose-bush to be planted for Auntie in the crematorium's Garden of Remembrance, and she was pruning it one gusty November Sunday (she visited the Garden every fortnight and preferred to look after the rose-bush herself as Auntie would have liked) when she fell into conversation with a gentleman performing the same task a bush or two away. His bush was newer than hers by several months; his wife had passed away only recently, he still wore a black band on his sleeve, and had hardly any idea of how to wield his secateurs.

Eunice showed him; she had a ruthless way of pruning which would, she knew, result in a mass of dainty blooms in summer. Mr Stafford – Stanley Stafford, retired Water Board official – was full of admiration. The wind was cold, his nose dripped slightly, he suggested a cup of tea.

Eunice had never considered marriage. She knew nothing of men save socially (married or semi-celibate around the Church Hall) or in business (often overbearing or unreasonable, with cigarette ash everywhere and not too careful about how they emerged from the toilet). As a television viewer and a client of the Public Library she had perforce had aspects of male behaviour presented to her; but television sets could be switched off, and although it was becoming more and more difficult to be sure no unpleasant antics or language appeared in novels, the librarians were fairly good by now at recommending those that might not offend, and there was always travel and biography – although even there one could no longer be sure nowadays, what with fertility rites and hitherto unpublished diaries.

No, men had never attracted her. They seemed, on the whole, selfish and dirty. But she did miss Auntie. Poor Mr Stafford was so pitiful, with his sad eyes and reddish nose, trying to look after himself in the rented flat he had shared with his late wife, the lease of which was nearly up. And there was she, lonely in Auntie's two-bedroomed house.

As a lodger? That would hardly be nice, people would talk . . .

They were married quietly in the spring. Eunice wore navy blue with touches of white and Mr Stafford wore a rose from his late wife's remembrance bush in his buttonhole. Eunice had made it quite clear from the beginning that there was to be none of 'that', and Mr Stafford had thankfully concurred. He was seventy-four and had never had much taste for it. He moved into Auntie's bedroom and Eunice remained in hers, and they never saw each other unless they were fully dressed. But he revelled in her competence, excellence and daintiness (his late wife had not been much of a housekeeper), in her cheerful small-talk, her tasteful presence alongside him in church or when viewing telly, and in the daintily delicious meals she set before him.

He was not used to them, and when they had been married less than a year he had a coronary thrombosis and died in Intensive Care.

Eunice was shocked. The arrangement had worked so well. Stanley had been no trouble, grateful for all she did, taking his own dirty clothes to the launderette so that she never had to handle them, giving up smoking so that there was no mess or fusty smell. He had praised her, comparing her favourably (but with good taste) with his late wife. He had been nearly as good as Auntie.

But better than Auntie in one way; he had left Eunice £9,000 and his life insurance policy. He had, surprisingly, turned out to be rather a good investment.

She missed him. Perhaps not exactly *him* but the appreciation he, like Auntie, had given her. Besides, now she was retired (she had resigned at marriage but in consideration of her twenty-seven years' service the organisation had not diminished her pension) she had very little to do. She would be willing – on the same terms, of course – to take on another man. And there seemed to be money in it . . .

The Garden of Remembrance was a lovesome thing, God wot, and Eunice continued to visit it as regularly as before, for she now had three rose-bushes to care for – Auntie, Stanley and Stanley's late wife (as she considered only nice). She observed the other visitors discreetly, and if a funeral were taking place would find out who was the deceased. If it was a gentleman she took no further action. But if it was a lady she would slip into a pew at the back of the chapel and take discreet part. Afterwards she joined the mourners to view the floral tributes and, some months after Stanley's death, stood in line to press the widower's hand and murmur, 'I was a friend of your wife's.'

'Oh yes – thank you,' he said, dazed, a small, bald man in a well-cut suit, his relatives prosperous-looking.

'Perhaps, when your grief has eased, I might call on you? So many happy memories . . .'

'Thank you. So kind.'

She pressed his hand and moved on. She knew who he was from the cards, his address would be in the telephone book.

This time it took longer, about eighteen months; and this time she sold Auntie's house and moved into Kenneth Gratton's handsome semi-detached on the Cliff Road. The arrangement was as before: separate rooms and no intimacies. But Kenneth was not otherwise at all the same as poor Stanley had been. He had been head of a building firm and used to ordering men about and getting his own way. Although he was small and bronchitic he had a will of concrete, drank whisky in the evening, refused to give up his pipe, which made the whole house smell disgusting as well as leaving dottles of burned tobacco in every dainty ashtray and even on the floor. He expected her to watch Match of the Day and, horror of horrors, wrestling. He disliked made-up dishes, dainties of every kind; liked fried onions, pickles and stout.

It was no hardship at all for Eunice to slip a sleeping-pill or two into his bedtime whisky and, when he was snoring loudly, place a pillow over his face.

Kenneth did not leave her his house (he left that to his son who lived in Newcastle and took no interest in his father's affairs) but he left her a reasonable sum – not as much as she had expected but she realised that Kenneth had been an error of judgment in many ways, something of a disappointment altogether. But there was always tomorrow, and pressing yet another widower's hand the following autumn she felt her instincts could be relied on this time.

Gilbert Phelps was pale, frail and asthmatic, almost unbecomingly eager for someone to continue taking care of him. He ate little and worried about his health and was, in fact, a very poor companion, although he possessed some sound investments and a house in the best part of Seaham which she sold at a good profit as soon as Probate was granted; it had been a happy release for them both.

Now, on the whole, she thought it would be wise to move from Seaham and start afresh elsewhere. She moved further along the coast, into a genteel private hotel, found the local Garden of Remembrance and a neglected rose-tree, and in not too long a time became Mrs Reginald Crocker, with a nice first-floor flat overlooking the promenade and a husband who was eighty-four years old.

No one was surprised when he apparently died in his sleep.

As Mrs Christine Crocker, Eunice married the following year a retired solicitor called Wilfred Jessop, who left her some more useful stocks and shares and property in Cornwall. This she sold, and with the proceeds bought herself a luxury bungalow (but big enough for two) in Redcliff-on-Sea where, as Christine Jessop, she became the wife of Bernard Barnes, company director and diabetic, whom she nursed daintily till his peaceful passing during the night not very long afterwards.

Redcliff-on-Sea had a large population of senior citizens, and before long, as Hilda Barnes, she married an ex-Army man, Major Desmond Heath. She found him crying under the pergola of the Garden of Remembrance, shame-faced into a large handkerchief, and, as with the first, harmless Stanley, gave him comfort and accepted a cup of tea.

The Major was small and stringy; he had served under Monty at Alamein and liked to tell stories of how sometimes, at first glance, he had been taken for that great warrior, standing sharp and keen in his jeep, battle-browned soldiers cheering his passing.

'Great days, marvellous days!' he would say, take out his handkerchief and blow his nose.

He and his late wife had been living in one of Redcliff's more expensive hotels. 'Never seemed to put down roots anywhere,' he said, 'Army life, rolling stones. Eleanor –' he gulped a little, as he always did in those early days at the mention of his late wife's name, 'Eleanor was content to be an Army wife – camp follower, I used to tease her. Longed for a home though sometimes, both of us. Home is the soldier, home from the lea, and the hunter home from the hill. We were looking around, but then – left it too late.'

He absolutely agreed with Eunice's provisos. 'Companionship, that's what you and I are about, isn't it, Hilda? Grow old along o' me. And to tell you the truth, that wound I got at Mersah Matruh . . .' He coughed, embarrassed, and Eunice changed the subject.

The Major moved in and they settled down in a way now very familiar to Eunice. As a military man, used to being on the move, he was sparse and neat in his belongings, orderly in his habits. He did not smoke, drank only one gin and tonic before supper, enjoyed gardening and the same television programmes that she did. His late wife had left him comfortably off and, what with one thing and another, Eunice had accumulated an extremely tidy sum over the recent years. The Major had a sweet tooth and appreciated her cakes and dainties. He paid her little compliments, which none of the others since Stanley had done; but chivalrous compliments, with no nasty suggestive undertone.

She really was getting to like the Major very much. He was a perfect gentleman. If this was marriage, she could begin to see why so many people recommended it: companionship, appreciation, nothing messy or disagreeable, privacy and respect, nothing that wasn't nice. She really felt she might settle for this one; marriage with the Major, growing old along o' him, no more speculative attendances at unknown funeral services, no more business prospects to consider, for surely the two of them had

112

quite enough between them to live comfortably to the end of their days?

She was very surprised, therefore, to be wakened in the middle of a night some months after their marriage by her bedroom door being opened and footsteps padding across the floor.

'Desmond? Is that you? What on earth . . . ?'

But he made no reply. And even if he had she wouldn't have heard it, for the pillow he pressed down on her face blanked out for ever all senses save terror and panic and an outraged incredulity.

*

What's to become of the pussies?

*

'Well, thank you, I don't mind if I do. I'll have a small gin and It and my friend'll have the same, I shouldn't wonder? This is my friend Mrs Martin and I'm Mrs Binns. We always come in here of a Tuesday, don't we, and have a little tipple – that's what we call it, our little tipple. It's Pension day, you see, dear, so we give ourselves a little treat while we're in funds, see? Us and the pussies.

You don't know about the pussies? Oh, my goodness, everyone around here knows about our pussies – down on the building site, well, it was waste ground really, you see, for years, after they cleared the bomb damage. And the poor little pussies what was strays, they started to live there, see, all in among the old cellars and bushes and that. What they lived on I don't know till me and Amy come along – shocking, it is, what people will leave their animals to, they ought to be hung. Half starved they were, and all the poor little kittens they went on having so bravely, bless 'em, mewing their little hearts out, and wild . . . ! You couldn't come near them, they'd be off in a flash, all in among the bricks and rubbish, and they'd watch you, see, with their little eyes all staring, like miniature tigers, weren't they, Amy? Ooh, they was sweet!

The building site? Yes, that's the one. Civic Centre or something it's going to be when it's done. But what Amy and me wants to know is, what's to become of the pussies? People don't think, you know. There's fewer there already than there was before all the building, and they'd all be waiting for us, bless their hearts. They knew us, you see, after we started going there regular. We'd go in careful all among the weeds and rubbish – you had to watch where you was going, you could have had a nasty fall in all that lot

114

if you wasn't careful – and we'd call Kitty kitty kitty kitty! and rustle a bit of newspaper and before you knew where you were they'd be round you. They seemed to come up out of the ground. Course, some of them'd never come close, they was too wild and fearful. They'd just crouch there, watching, and then when we'd put their dinners down they'd sort of stretch out slinking along the ground, ever so cautious and nervy, and snatch up the food and run off with it. That was at first, wasn't it, Amy, but after a bit they'd stay there and eat it, but ever so watchful, goodness, their eyes darting every which way and their tails twitching, and growling all the time . . . Ooh, it was a picture!

Course, those was the wild ones. The ones that hadn't been there so long, they was tamer. They used to run up to us, didn't they, Amy, with their little tails up like signposts, mewing and purring, rubbing round our legs – ooh, they knew who their friends were all right, bless 'em, the little sweethearts! Sometimes there'd be as many as ten or twelve all weaving round our feet, and the other ones watching a bit farther off. And then we'd put them each out their bits of dinner, all on separate bits of newspaper, see, and we'd say Now, kitty, that's for you and this one's for you, and we'd space them out nicely, see, so each had his own special place, and I think I can truthfully say we never had no more than a spit and a growl sometimes once they'd got used to what we was doing. They knew we was friends, see, bless 'em, even the wild ones. Ooh, it was a lovely sight, it really was, especially of a summer's evening – we used to go down about seven o'clock, after the traffic was quieter, see. All those dear little pussies tucking into their dinners all among the weeds and the broken bricks and the old tyres and rubbish in the evening sunshine – ooh, it was a picture, I can tell you.

Every day we went, but Tuesdays was special because of the Pension. We used to get them a nice bit of lovely fresh mince on Tuesdays, didn't we, Amy. Ooh, they did love their mince! And you could see the good it did them, too – some of them got quite plump and their coats got a shine on them and they looked like proper pussies again, bless their poor little hearts – ooh, it makes us wild to think what people will do to poor helpless animals, absolutely wild! You can't tell me they'd ever leave a good home and live rough like that of their own accord. It's all these tower blocks as is causing it. People just can't keep animals in them, see, even if they was allowed, and so they just turn the poor sweethearts out in the streets to fend for themselves with never a thought. Wicked it is, proper wicked! And then the boys go in, playing their nasty rough games in the waste ground, throwing stones and scaring them half to death, tin cans and I don't know what-all. Ooh, I gave them what-for when I caught them rampaging, I can tell you – little hooligans! Course, it's the parents I blame. No discipline, that's what's the trouble. Scared of their own kids. You show me a bad boy and I'll show you a bad parent, isn't that right, Amy? We was brought up to respect other people, look after the little ones. My dad'd take his slipper to me if I didn't look after the little ones.

Well, thank you, dear, that's ever so kind of you. The same again, if that's convenient. My, Amy, this is a treat and no mistake! I was only saying to Amy this evening, I said My goodness, I could do with a bit of a treat this evening, I said, didn't I, Amy? You see, we was both feeling a bit down this evening. Yes, well, you see we've not been able to feed our pussies this evening – nor yesterday neither, you see, with all the police about. I don't know what our pussies will think. I don't like to think about it. They've come to rely on us, see – nearly two years we've been going, regular as clockwork, summer and winter – and not very nice it was sometimes in the winter, I can tell you, rain and gales and black as pitch and ever so treacherous underfoot. But we always went, didn't we, Amy? We used to say Those poor little sweethearts has more to put up with than us, we said, we've got nice warm homes to go to and they haven't, we said, and ooh, they was grateful! Picking their way through the mud to us on their poor little paws, mewing fit to break your heart, creeping up out of all the little holes and crannies of shelter they'd found for theirselves . . . But now we don't know what they'll do, not with everything all sealed off and nasty great police officers all over everything. I said to the constable on the gate – you know, where the tractors go in and the fence is all bashed down – I said, What'll happen to all our pussies, I said, they rely on us, I said, and he simply gave me a sarky look and said If you want to leave your footprints all over the scene of the crime, Ma, he said, you go right ahead. Course, I didn't answer him, cheeky young fellow. My dad'd soon have sorted him out.

Well, yes, it's not very nice. Shocking, you might say. I'm sorry for the men who turned him up, it can't have been very nice. Course, we don't know much more than what's in the papers. He don't seem to've been nobody. I mean, they know what his name was and that, but they haven't got no more than that. Nasty piece of work, he was. One of them gangsters, I shouldn't be surprised – you know, shooting each other outside public houses and that, shocking. I said to Amy, I said I bet he's one of them gangsters, didn't I, Amy? They're in all kinds of nastiness, I said, and one's as bad as the other. I mean, you'd only got to look at him to see he was no good – you've seen his photo in the papers, I expect.

Course, he's been there some time. It's wonderful what the police can find out nowadays when you wouldn't hardly think there'd be anything left to go on. I mean, it's not very nice, but it is wonderful, when you come to think of it. I mean, they know who he was and where he come from and how long he's been there and I suppose they'll find out if he drowned or not once them police doctors get busy on him. I wish them joy of him, that's all I can say. Nasty sort of job for a decent man to choose, I always think, mucking about in dead bodies. Quite turns me up.

Well now, I shouldn't really. Really I shouldn't. Well, if you're sure. Well, just a little one. Oh, go on Amy – be a teenage rebel. That's what some saucy young chap said to me once in the street. Be a teenage rebel, he said – I had to laugh. Oh, well, if she won't she won't, it's no good pressing her. Obstinate as a mule, Amy is, once she's made up her mind to a thing you can't budge her. I'm not like that. I'm impulsive. Like when you first sat down here and got into conversation, I took to you. Yes I did, dear, I took to you or I'd never have started talking about our pussies.

Course, he's not the first, you know. Oh, no there's another one in there somewhere. They'll come across him, I suppose, now they've got those great big bulldozers digging it all up – ugly great things, aren't they, not like the cranes. I like the cranes, they've got a kind look. You look out of your window and look up at the sky and there they are, all yellow and orange like some great big giraffe or something, moving about up there, and all the red and yellow clay down below and the grey huts and the men with their red helmets and the yellow patches on their coats and the broken bits of houses they're knocking down over the other side . . . I tell you, it's a real picture in a funny sort of way, specially on a fine morning. And at night, with the light shining out on the cranes up there in the sky, like angels' wings, I say to myself – angels' wings. Yes, I do, Amy, some of us has imagination. Angels' wings hovering over our pussies, I'd say.

They did find one. It never got into the papers, of course, for it wasn't of any importance. I mean, it was only a nasty old meths drinker nobody knew – they used to sleep rough out there in the summer when it was just waste ground, build fires and drink themselves silly. It really wasn't very nice, I can tell you. Me and Amy was plumb scared once or twice, and the pussies used to streak away like greased lightning and no wonder! You wouldn't believe what we found he was doing – I mean, we all know they've not got two pennies to rub together, but there's all sorts of places they can get some sort of a meal, shelters and hostels and the Salvation Army. I mean, there's no excuse . . .

Stop nudging me, Amy. What's got into you? It's no good looking at me old-fashioned, we're all friends here. If you ask me, that gin and It's disagreed with you. If I was you I'd go off quick to the toilet, you look a bit green round the gills. You'd better make haste, dear, before you feel it all coming up . . . That's right, you go off, it's over there on the right . . .

She can't hold it, you see, not spirits. She's got a delicate stomach, always has had. She'll feel better after she's been. The least thing out of the way upsets her – she was like this after we went back next day and found him still there. Well, we didn't

118

know what to do. White as a sheet she was and shaking, but never got rattled. She's a cool head on her shoulders, Amy has, despite her digestion. Well, I said, we can't just leave him here. Think of the pussies, I said, it's not very nice. He'd knocked his head, you see, falling into the cellar, and – well, you can imagine. But Amy said That's just what we will do, she said, and what with one thing and another I think he'll get taken care of. Some young lads found him in the end, on one of their rampages – it must have given them a turn.

Course, we didn't go back there, not to that particular spot, not after that. We went to another place, and the pussies soon cottoned on and followed us, bless their clever little hearts.

My word, there were a lot that summer! Beauties some of them were, sleek and fat as anything thanks to Amy and me. I used to say I'd like to take some of them home with us, but of course, we couldn't do that, they was too wild really, even the tame ones, and anyway you can't keep cats in a bed-sit, can you, it'd be cruel. But ooh, we were proud of some of them, proper tigers they were, fit to win prizes. We couldn't believe our senses when we found some of them missing. We called and called, and the other ones never turned up, and we couldn't think what had become of them, and then . . . Ooh, I can hardly bear to think of it even now – and that's over nine months ago! There he was, bold as brass, as nasty a piece of work as ever you saw. Crouched down, he was, with a paper of fried fish in one hand and a great big net in the other – you know, like what we used to go shrimping with when we was kiddies. My dad and me used to have lovely shrimp teas when I was a kiddie, down at my granny's place at Bexhill. But don't they make your hands smell nasty?

Well, dear, we was ever so careful after that. I mean, it wouldn't bear thinking of, our lovely pussies used for that! We used to feel quite sick that winter whenever we saw some silly young girl all bundled up in a fun fur – that's what they call them, fun furs, would you believe it? I'd fun them if ever I had the chance – all our lovely pussies we'd taken such a pride in! We was careful never to go there after that till it was getting dark, and we'd spy out whether there was strangers about or people we didn't like the look of. But no, it was all peaceful again and we thought we'd seen the end of it, and Amy said it just went to show you had to stick up for yourself and the poor little innocents. They seemed to know. Ever so loving and tame they got, even the wild ones in their own funny way – sitting and staring and sometimes they'd just let you stroke their dear little heads for a minute – but of course, you had to be careful, bless 'em, or they'd give it a claw.

And then, blow me if one evening we didn't find the very same thing again! Mind you, we'd been warned. There's been ever such a lot in the papers just now about cat thieves, hasn't there, so of course we'd been keeping our eyes open. But you know how it is, you never think that sort of thing will happen in your own place, do you? I mean, it's inhuman, isn't it, you just couldn't credit it that anyone could be so downright wicked. So when Amy and me got there and saw this beast bending down over his net with one of our pussies – Queenie, it was, she'd had three litters already this year, the sweetheart, and always the same, two black and two ginger – well, I just went wild. You beast, I yelled out, and he jumped like he'd been shot, for he hadn't heard us coming up behind him. You filthy beast, I said, what're you doing to our pussies? I said. Ooh, he was a nasty shifty piece of work all right! He straightened up and looked us right in the eye and he said, I don't believe I'm doing anything to your pussies, darling, and Amy said, We don't want none of your nasty talk, young man, you clear out of it, and he said – and he used a filthy expression, dear – I'll do what I – ing well like with these – ing pussies. And, well, I just saw red again, just like I had those other times. I upped with me arm and I gave him a great big swipe with me handbag – you can see it's a big one, dear, and it was full of tins of cat food at the time – and I caught him such a clout across the earhole that he staggered back. And as he was staggering back Amy shot her shopping-trolley out behind him – it had the pussies cartons of milk in it and some halibut oil, they do love halibut oil – and he went arse over tip, if you'll pardon my French, on to his backside. I suppose he must have been a bit stunned by it all, for quick as a

flash Amy whipped out the big plastic bag we carry the fish in –
only it wasn't fish that day, you see, but Kattipur, so it was empty –
and she whipped it over his head and down over his shoulders and
gave it a sort of twist while he was sort of floundering and coming
to, and then we give him a great big shove and splash! he went into
the puddle – well, more of a pond really, it's been a shocking wet
autumn, hasn't it, and some of them holes and the old foundations
have got really deep, dangerous really for kiddies playing about.
Of course, they can't do that now, not now they've started the
building.

Ah, here's Amy back again. You look a bit better now, dear, I
must say. Are you feeling all right? That's good. I was just saying,
the kiddies can't play on the waste ground no more, not now
they've started the building.

But what'll become of our pussies? We didn't reckon on them
starting the building, you see, not till the spring. If they'd left it till
the spring it'd have been all right, you see, what with the weather
and one thing and another. But as it is – well, I just don't know.
We've been up there this evening and left some bits and pieces out
near the fence, but the poor little sweethearts won't know where
to find it, not being their usual place and all those policemen
tramping all over everywhere. And goodness knows there'll be
even more of them when they turn up the other one . . .

Oh, my goodness, Amy, what a face! I tell you, you've got to be
careful of Amy when she looks like that, old-fashioned's not in it!
Oh well, smile and shame the devil, I say. We'll just have to wait
and see what happens, won't we, Amy?'

Amy said nothing.

*

Moon daisy

*

We kept no end of state at Brettenham (pronounced Bretham by those in the know). There must be more than twenty indoor servants and heaven knows how many on the estate, not counting the home farm. In the autumn, when they have house parties for the shooting and each guest brings his own servants, the place must be like a medieval court; and if the Prince and Princess of Wales graciously consent to drive over from Sandringham for a day's sport – my word, what splendour!

Mind you, I've not seen this myself – I had it from Miss Tiffen, the Family's seamstress. She used to be the children's nurse, but now they are all grown up and away – the girls well married, the boys serving the Empire at various far-flung outposts – she sits all day in one of the tower rooms, mending and altering and stitching, a little bent old woman with eyes as bright as a robin's. She knows everything about the Family; but she tells only what redounds to their glory and credit. The bad things she keeps silent about – as I found in the end.

I spent a fair bit of time with Miss Tiffen. She, like myself, had no fixed place in the household, she by reason of age and long intimacy with the Family which made her now more than a servant but of course much less than a friend, and I because although I am as gently bred as Lord Brettenham himself (probably more so, for he is only the third baron whereas my father could trace our line back to at least the seventeenth century, yeomen gentry who threw up scholars from time to time but lacked the venality to make their way in the world) I was at Brettenham only as an employee, filling the three summer months by cataloguing Lord Brettenham's library and family papers. And glad indeed to do so,

122

for funds were exceedingly low until September, when I was to take up an appointment as junior master in a school for the sons of clergymen in Blackheath.

The cataloguing was tedious; the Family's interests seem, for their short but swift rise from mercantile obscurity, to have been almost entirely political and sporting, their papers accounts and meticulously kept game-books, their library political and theological. I worked each day alone in the library, my luncheon brought to me by the under-parlourmaid. Breakfast I took alone in the old schoolroom, tea usually with Miss Tiffen, once I discovered her existence. Dinner again alone in the schoolroom – unless, ah unless! the Family found themselves a gentleman short at the dinner table, in which case, by means of a note brought to me by a footman, I would be bidden to make up the requisite number; to take in, it might be, the spinster sister of the Rector (themselves invited merely to fill the lower reaches of the table well below the salt) or some tongue-tied daughter of a local squire invited to soften his reluctance to having his crops trampled flat by being shot over, even by Royal Highnesses.

On these occasions, arrayed in the formal black and white which had been my father's, I would make my way down the many staircases into the great hall with its fireplaces banked with potted plants, to the drawing room, its floor a hazardous ice-rink beneath costly rugs, its chandeliers a-twinkle despite the evening sun – the better, perhaps, to display the satins and brocades, the jewelled dog-collars, tiaras, parures, earrings as large, it seemed, as the chandeliers themselves, that glittered on the ladies of the swells therein assembled.

'Ah, Mr Fisher,' his lordship would drawl agreeably if he happened to notice my arrival, 'how's the work progressing, heh? Mr Fisher's our bookworm, heh?' to whoever stood nearest us.

'Very well, sir, I think.'

'Capital, capital,' and that would be the end of it. Before dinner was announced milady would glide up to me, a-rustle with taffeta, a-twinkle with gems. Tapping me on the arm with her fan, she would instruct me as to which hapless female I was to take in and waft me to her side. She, poor creature, seldom knew who I was, and I not often she. Throughout the interminable meal we would try and make conversation of a kind.

When the ladies left us and the port circulated I was in limbo. I did my best, but my neighbours soon gave me up as a bad job. Politics, racing and risqué stories did not interest me, cigars make me feel ill, and I do not care for drink or drunkards; and when blessed release came I did not go with the others to join the ladies but made my way out through the billiard room on to the terrace, to breathe in the purity and silence of the night. No one would miss me; my function had been solely to fill an empty place.

Brettenham is very beautiful, especially on a fine summer night. The house stands four-square, rather grey and bleak, on a platform backed by ancient trees. Behind the trees, beyond the park, lie the heath and woodlands over which the Family shoot, but facing down a gentle slope of parkland (beyond which, many miles away, lies the sea) the mansion seems to survey limitless tranquillity, a harmony of grassland, trees and lake.

It is the lake which gives the grace and focus to the landscape, tree-edged in places, at others fringed with reeds, and in the day constantly a-shimmer with duck and wildfowl of all kinds, clucking and preening, rising with a sharp rustle of wings as though a hundred umbrellas were suddenly opened, descending again with a long splashing wake to resettle wing and breast feathers – which feathers bestrew the grass and small beaches of the lakeside like confetti. It was my delight sometimes to gather them up into airy posies, as many different kinds as I could find, and take them to Miss Tiffen.

But at night the lake seemed spellbound. Dark in the darkness, utterly still between its reeded banks – and yet never still, always stealthily alive with wind sounds, water sounds, the small movements of water rat and vole, the stirring, breathing of birds that only seemed to sleep, muttering, chuckling, preening in the darkness, making their own silence in the secrecy of the night.

I came out on to the side terrace nearest the lake that evening of the dinner, my lungs sour with cigar smoke, my ears with the blare and blather of the swells, my heart filled with bitter loneliness and – yes – self-pity. What was I doing here, ignored or patronised by these moneyed boobies? I was a scholar. That was why I was here, recommended by my father's friend and lawyer when it was found my father had left nothing. That same recommendation would start me as a schoolmaster in two months' time, a prospect I dreaded, for although I am a scholar, it is as a writer that I wish to make my name. Was this to be my life? At twenty-two, was I already doomed to drudgery and subservience?

From the open windows of the mansion behind me I could hear music, a woman singing, the tepid clatter of gloved applause. I went down the steps and across the grass to the lakeside.

It was a still, clear night, a new moon steadfast in the sky. Sunk in my doleful thoughts I wandered with bent head along the bank; the music fell away behind me, the blessed silence enshrouded me, calmed me. And then, pale in the starlight, I saw a girl standing at the edge of the reeds.

My heart gave a thump, for she looked like a ghost standing there quite still by the water's edge, swathed in some pale material, gazing away from me down the far side of the lake. Then I realised that the paleness came from a bibbed, encompassing apron, her hair (pale in itself) partly covered by a frilled white cap. My heart resumed normal beating and I said jokingly, 'I took you for a ghost.'

She gave a start and turned her face towards me. 'I didn't hear you, sir.'

'Did I frighten you?'

'No. I don't frighten easy.' Her voice was soft, with a faint Norfolk twang.

'It's a fine night.'

'Aye.' She turned to look down the lake again, indifferent to me Piqued, I stayed where I was.

'Are you from the house?'

'Aye.' She faced me again. It was a pale, composed face, the mouth firm, the eyes steady. The wide starched bands on the

125

shoulders of her apron seemed to reflect light. 'I'm one of the housemaids.'

'I've not seen you about.'

'You wouldn't.'

Her lack of 'sir' stung me. 'I'm from the house too,' I said grandly.

'Aye, you must be else you wouldn't be here.' A faint smile touched her mouth. She was like no servant I had met yet – perhaps because we were out here in the night alone, away from the rigid hierarchy of the mansion.

On impulse I asked, 'What's your name?'

'Daisy.'

'Daisy. A moon daisy.'

'If you like. Sir.' She was definitely smiling now, a soft teasing smile.

'Do you often come here in the dark?'

'Sometimes. When there's time.'

'I also. I shall look for you again.'

'Likely you will.' She began to move away, the reeds hazing the pale glimmer of her garments.

I called, 'Yes, you may be sure of it.'

Her voice had laughter in it. 'Sleep well. Sir.' And she was gone.

She must have known I would not sleep well – her voice had promise of it. But it was sleeplessness with pleasure in it. She haunted me. I kept seeing the glimmer of her face and figure, hearing the cool teasing of her voice. Her lack of servility piqued me; she knew I was a gentleman from my speech and manner. I had been dressed in evening togs too; and, as she had said, how else would I be there, strolling at ease by Brettenham's lake of a summer evening after a grand dinner party? Where in the house did she work, I wondered, why had I never seen her? But there were dozens of servants I never saw in that huge establishment; they were expertly trained to be invisible.

I tried Miss Tiffen, roundabout. 'It's such a grand household, ma'am, I've never seen the like. How many indoor servants would there be? – how many housemaids, say?'

'What's it to you, Mr Fisher?'

'Nothing. Curiosity. I thought I heard someone calling for "Daisy" in the upstairs corridor this morning, that's all.'

She gave me a sharp look. 'Daisy? No Daisy here, you can depend on that. And there should be no calling in the passage of Brettenham House. What impudence!' Well, she was old and seldom left her attic rooms; she would hardly know the names of all the staff.

Each evening if it were fine – and that summer it mostly was – I took to sauntering down to the lakeside after my dinner. I soon grew used to the darkness, and in any case the moon was waxing. I wandered round the lake, my eyes searching for the girl's pale figure, but for some nights I did not find her. Then, there she was, standing in the same reeded place, looking away down the lake.

'Daisy?'

She turned. 'Ah, 'tis you, sir.'

'Yes.'

'I thought that might be.'

I was disconcerted. 'You did, did you? Why was that?'

'That'd be telling. Let's say, because you wanted to.'

'And you?'

She laughed, and I felt not only my blood but my heart begin to pound.

'I'm only a servant,' she said. 'That don't matter what I want.'

'And what do you want?'

'Oh . . .' She let the word hang in the silence for a moment. 'I want to be like them.' She nodded towards the house, where lights blazed from every window. 'I want to wear fine clothes and a jewel or so and have someone else to do my washing and make my bed. I want to see London and look at the Queen.'

'London's not much of a place.'

Her voice sharpened. 'You shouldn't say that. That's not what

127

they say. You should say 'tis a fine place and you'll take me there. You should say if I go with you to London you'll give me fine clothes and a carriage and make me a lady.'

'I can't say that. It wouldn't be true.'

'Yes you must, 'tis what they all say. You're no different.' She began to move away.

'I am, Daisy. I am different.'

'You're a gentleman, aren't you, from the house?'

'Yes, but . . .'

'Won't you take me to London, then?' She was still leaving me, her voice teasing yet plaintive.

'Yes, yes if I can. If you want . . . but why?'

'That's right. That's what you must say. That's the way of it. Sir.'

She was gone.

Even now, I cannot understand what madness seized me. I was distracted. I no longer knew whether I stood on my head or my heels. I seemed to have gone mad, to have become possessed by a girl I did not know, could never know save in impurity, a servant I had not even touched, a country girl of unknown background, shameless, unscrupulous – but magical, magnetic, all-pervading. My dreams were full of her – hot, shameful, exhausting dreams; my day thoughts turned again and again to her from the dry cataloguing of the Family's effects. I know now that I was in fact bewitched, but then it merely seemed to me that I had at last found, in that barren waste of condescension and indifference, someone who spoke and responded to me on equal terms – more, a lovely being who treated me as a woman treats a man, teasing, promising, tender. Yet not quite as an equal; impudent though she was, she spoke to me as to a man of power and breeding, a swell who could take her up on a whim and translate this country wanton into a town dolly. I, who had no influence, no wealth, no home! It was this that turned my head, as though I were indeed a lord, her master. I was drunk with the power of it – and with her strange, pale beauty, the provocation that weighted her voice and her words.

I slipped out every evening down to the lake to see if she was there. The weather had turned, the trees stirred and threshed in the wind, the moon was obscured by cloud. She did not come. I walked through the quaggy edge of the lakeside where the reeds were as high as my shoulders, but she was not there. In ten days' time my employment would be over, the archives and the library in order, listed in heavy leather tomes that no one, I judged, would ever glance at. I should be paid my fee by the steward: perhaps her ladyship might condescend to wish me farewell and his lordship to express satisfaction and the promise of a reference should any of his acquaintances require my services. And I should be driven to the station in the dogcart with my portmanteau and return to London and some dreary lodging, to sweat out the August heat before setting forth again to that unknown school whose general dogsbody I would be.

No! In a ruthless world why should I not be ruthless too? Why should I not do as Daisy urged, take her with me and enjoy if only for a time the solace of her charms? If she was so reckless as to trust herself to a man she hardly knew, I would be mad enough to accept that trust. London she wanted and London she should have!

Calm, rich nights came again, the winds blown out. As I kept my vigil I heard only the secret stir of lakeside life. The moon, now full and tinged with gold, sailed huge in the huge sky.

She was there. Her head was bare tonight, the pale hair shining in two smooth wings either side of her face, caught back in an old-fashioned knot, a few tendrils escaping by her ears, infinitely seductive.

She turned when I spoke her name. 'Ah, 'tis you. I knew you'd come.'

'I've looked for you each night.'

'Aye. That's full moon now. Sweethearts' time.'

'Daisy.' I took a step towards her along the narrow path. 'I leave next week. Back to London.'

Her eyes glittered. 'You'll take me?'

'Yes.'

'Ah!' She drew in her breath and smiled, not at me but up into the glow of the moon. 'You want me bad, eh? You'll take me up and set me up, like all the gentlemen say? But you'll not get nothing till we're safe in London. I'm not to be tumbled under the trees and then left to watch you drive off in your carriage and pair. London's my price, my fine gentleman – nothing before!'

Her words shocked me; and yet, in their challenging impudence I sensed a desperate fear. Despite the harshness of her manner, the provocation of her movements as she swayed a step or two away from me, there seemed terror and, yes, innocence. The face she turned to me as she moved was that of a child – a knowing child but one moved by bravado; fearful, uncertain, yet determined.

I took a step or two after her, the path squelching beneath my feet. 'Daisy,' I said, 'it's not like that.'

'London's my price,' she said. 'You'll not see or touch before you've bought the goods. I'll have no gentleman's tricks from you.'

She had retreated further among the reeds and I followed her. 'It's not like that,' I said again. 'I'm not what you think. I'm not a swell, I'm not a guest up at the house.'

'You're a gentleman,' she repeated.

'Yes. But not as you mean. I'm not rich. I've no money save what I earn and that's little enough, and I'm only a sort of a lackey up at the house, at work in the library. I'm not one of the Family's set, I'm no one.'

'You must be.' Her voice was uncertain now. 'You're up at the house, in fine clothes and all, dining with all the nobs. You speak soft and fine and you're hot for a servant girl, like all of them is.'

'Daisy, no! You're mistaken, gravely mistaken. I'm not a nob,

I'm no one. I'll take you to London and if you stay with me I'll treat you with all the respect I can. But there's no carriage and no fine clothes – only an honest heart and no lies between us.'

I went further towards her, for I wanted to take her by the hand and let her see in my face that I spoke the truth; that we'd go together, I'd keep my word, but as comrades, lovers I hoped in time, but without falsehood.

But she shrank away before me, her face bewildered. 'No!' she cried, 'that's not how 'tis. You're a gentleman, rich, and you want your will of me now, like a slut in a barn. That's all lies about going to London, you want me now and leave me, ruin me here and nothing to pay! That's how 'tis, that's how it always is!'

'Daisy, no! I'll not touch you. I'm not what you think. I'm poor, Daisy, like you . . .' I thrust nearer to her, though the reeds closed in on me and I felt the mud oozing up through my thin shoes. The reeds rustled around me and small sounds came from creatures disturbed by our presence. As I plunged towards her she threw out her hands as though to fend me off and her face, retreating before me, was whiter than ever in the steadfast beam of the moon.

'No, no!' she cried. 'Go back! That's wrong – that's all mazed and wrong! You're not the one it should be – you're like my Jed, my darling . . .' Then she raised her face to the sky and cried in a voice so raw with loss and anguish that my heart went cold, 'They hung my darling! They hung my Jed! Go back, you're not the one – go back, go back . . .'

I felt the lake water rise above my ankles, calves, knees. I blundered towards her but she seemed always to recede before me, gliding backwards through the reeds that scratched and tore at my face and hands, her face a mask of fear and, it seemed, pity, her pale hands waving me back, back, as she fled, faded, hung above the water like a shimmering mist as I tripped and fell face downward in the knotted weeds and reeds and quagmire of the lakeside, felt the water close over me, tasted the mud in my mouth, heard her voice echoing, 'Go back, go back – you're not the one . . .'

A woodman found me as he went to work soon after the sun rose. I was lying in the mud at the lake's edge, half submerged but with my face and head somehow pulled clear of the water. I was unconscious and they got a hurdle and carried me back to the house, where I gather my condition caused something of a stir. Vaguely I was aware of bustle around my bedside, voices, even her ladyship's, and someone saying with great emphasis, 'This is the third, I tell you!' I drifted and dozed, at last returning to myself at evening, the curtains drawn, a lamp shaded on the dressing-table, and old Miss Tiffen seated at my bedside, her gnarled hands in her lap, her eyes shut.

I stirred and at once her lids were open and her bright old eyes regarded me. 'Ah,' she said, 'you return to us. How do you feel?'

'Very hot.'

'Naturally. You have three blankets and a coverlet and a hot brick at your feet. I will remove that now, but you have suffered a severe chill, lying out all night by the lake.' She rose and darted her arm under the bedclothes at my feet to extract the flannel-wrapped warmer. She placed it on the floor, reseated herself, and told me how I had been discovered, the reeds trampled down around me as though I had struggled to drag myself out of the lake. When she had done she folded her hands in her lap and studied me intently.

'And now,' she said, 'I should like to inquire how you got there?'

I told her. Shameful in many ways though my story was, I kept nothing back. Weakened alike by exposure and by emotion, I let the whole short but overwhelming record of my encounters with Daisy flood out of me, trying to convey to Miss Tiffen the strange magnetism of that moonlit creature and the bitter loneliness in myself which caused my, as I saw it now, incredible response.

Miss Tiffen listened in silence, nodding her lace-capped head now and then. When I had done she nodded again. 'Yes,' she said, 'it is as I thought.'

After a moment I said, 'I wish no harm to come to Daisy. She was not to blame.'

'No,' she said. 'It is the world that is to blame. Lust and ambition and the power of high personages are to blame.' She nodded twice. 'She should not be blamed for wanting to better herself.'

'She'll not be dismissed?'

She gave me a queer look. 'Young man,' she said, 'I will tell you for no one else in this house will, they fear the scandal. Daisy Hunter was murdered down by the lake some sixty years ago.' As I gasped she laid a hand firmly on mine. 'Stay still. I was the under-nurserymaid then, newly in service, fourteen years of age. We were friends of a sort. His lordship's father was the lord then. Daisy had a sweetheart, Jed Barber, a gamekeeper. She loved him, I'm sure, but she was eager to better herself and him, hot in the flesh as country girls are, not wise in the head. One of the old lord's friends caught sight of her, a foreign Highness, she took his fancy and she led him on. She was found drowned at the lakeside one full moon with marks on her throat, and it was Jed that found her and Jed they hanged for it.'

She was silent for a moment, her eyes looking into the past. Then she gave my hand a little pat again. 'There were another two found there over the years – gentlemen, friends of his lordship. Drowned in the mud at full moon, no one knew how or why. Their deaths were hushed up, of course. They could find no scapegoat for them as they had for Daisy's murder. He didn't hang, you see, it was all covered up by the Family. Wealth can do that. Poor Jed got the blame and was hanged for it. Yes, that's the way it was.'

'But – the others?'

'I think,' she said, and her voice was almost tender, 'I think poor Daisy's wanted revenge. It was Jed she loved, despite her grand ideas – we were bits of girls together, I knew her mind. She's had revenge and no one's lived to say how. But you've lived.'

'Why? Why me?'

She drew a handkerchief out from the pocket she kept hung under her skirt and blew her nose. Her eyes were brighter than ever I thought, with tears.

'She saw that you weren't a villain but just a silly young man. Not a lord of creation like those others had been, to take what you like and the rest of us all keep silence, but a simple, silly young person like herself – and Jed. You touched her heart, even though she's dead.' She blew her nose again and stuffed the handkerchief back under her skirts. 'Pity wipes out revenge. Daisy's gone now, I think.'

'Amen,' I said.

She covered my hand with hers. 'Amen. God rest their souls.'

And mine, I should have echoed; for the loss and loveliness haunt me to this day.

*

The better part of valour

*

This was the sixth year that Mrs Lambert and the Major had gone on holiday together. They had first met on a coach tour of Scotland; the Major, always nimble at getting aboard before anyone else, had chivalrously given her his own window-seat when, couples having possessed the double seats, the single passengers came bumping along the aisle seeking a haven. Thereafter he had always kept the window-seat for her, and stowed her raincoat up on the rack with his own. Thus *they* became a couple, with a couple's advantages. And, self-sufficient though Mrs Lambert had become, these were not negligible.

They found they both lived in south London, Mrs Lambert in Wimbledon, the Major in what he called his bachelor pad in Putney. Six weeks after their return from Scotland the Major invited her to be his lady at his regimental dinner-dance held annually at the Connaught Rooms. Mrs Lambert consented; and six weeks later invited him to partner her at her local bridge club. He was not a good player and she did not ask him again; but the pattern was formed, and once every six weeks or so he would invite her to a theatre and she would invite him to supper at her house, other people being present to make up a four.

It seemed natural that the following year they should repeat the holiday arrangement. This time they decided on a coach tour of the châteaux of the Loire, and very enjoyable it was. The next year it was Holland, the bulb fields allied to Franz Hals and the Rijksmuseum. Then came the Rhine, rather disappointing ('The Rhine maidens must have choked to death years ago,' observed Mrs Lambert); then Treasures of Italy, by air to Nice and thence a coach to Milan, Florence and Sienna. Exhausting, but with two of you so much easier and so very much worthwhile.

This year it was Greece.

They always made their own separate bookings. That way there was no embarrassment, financial or otherwise. Besides, the Major was apt to be a little slapdash, to take what the travel agents said on trust and not check times or schedules. As a soldier he expected his orders to be carried out and took an airy view of making sure – 'It's those fellers' job,' he said. 'They ought to know.' But Mrs Lambert always made sure and sometimes saved the Major if not from disaster at least from dismay. 'Chappie hadn't got me a reservation,' he'd say. 'Damned inefficient, but it's okay now.'

Mrs Lambert's accommodation was always slightly more expensive than the Major's, with a bathroom and a better view. 'I can doss down any old where,' he said, 'so long as the grub's up to scratch.' He was full of boyish gusto about food and drink, but in fact had a more delicate digestion than Mrs Lambert who, in her quiet way, consumed everything. But neither of them cared for alcohol, which spared them the embarrassment of who should pay for the drinks. Tips she allowed the Major to take care of – that, and luggage, was one of the advantages of travelling with a man. But on the rare occasions when they needed a taxi or an excursion not on the itinerary she insisted that she paid. 'You wouldn't be doing this but for me,' she'd say. 'You must allow me to treat myself to a small extravagance.' He would yield, but tip the driver with a prodigal air. Mrs Lambert suspected he had only his pension.

Whereas she had four houses in Raynes Park, six in Wandsworth, and the one she lived in, a semi-detached, semi-timbered 1920s-ish villa in what had been an almost country lane when she and John Lambert married in the 1930s. She had remained there after he died; the house suited her, although of course she did not need three bedrooms, having no children. An agent managed her properties but in fact she kept a close watch on everything, deciding when to sell and when to buy, when to redecorate or

136

convert or seek planning permission for an added amenity. She understood perfectly every aspect of the various Rent Acts and of Capital Gains, although her agent did not know this.

Nor did the Major. The Major knew nothing about her circumstances save that she had been a widow for some twenty-five years and owned her own house. He would never ask and she would never tell him, for although over the six years of their companionship they had grown closer they had not grown more intimate.

True, their meetings were now once a month or even every three weeks; and, true, she no longer always arranged that other people should be present when he came to supper. Often it was just the two of them, a simple meal and the lemon barley water she kept specially for him, and watching television afterwards. As he put on his coat and set off to walk first up, then down the hill to Putney ('Never use transport if Shanks's mare can take you,' he said, but perhaps it was partly to save fares) he often looked wistful; and latterly he had taken to holding her hand as they stood at the open front door, looking into her face with his bright blue eyes, and sighing. Once or twice he had even kissed her hand, blushed, jammed his tweed hat on his head and bolted down the path. No reference was ever made to these occasions. She behaved as though they had not happened, although the place where his moustache had pressed seemed to stay hot and moist for several moments.

She knew that at the slightest relaxation of her habitual neutrality something might burst from him. She had known this for quite a long time. He would dare nothing without a sign from her. Somewhat to her surprise, she had lately begun to consider giving that sign.

The coach party spent their first night in a noisy hotel off Omonia Square. As was his custom, the Major made it clear at Reception and to the hotel lobby in general that his room was on the fourth floor while that of Mrs Lambert was on the first, which came as a surprise to other members of the party who had assumed, since they had travelled self-sufficiently together from London, that this round, bald man and his neat companion were man and wife.

The party consisted of what at first glance appeared to be the identical people who had been on all the other coach trips back over the years: the elderly couples; the pairs of middle-aged female friends; the several young or older single women; the three single men, two old and widowed, one youngish and lissome. Everything had gone smoothly so far, except that two singles had been booked into a double, and a tartan hold-all belonging to a large single lady was missing. While search was made its owner, Miss Fordyce, stood lamenting in the middle of the lobby, her hair in wisps, her cardigan slipping from her uneven shoulders. The bag was found still in the coach, and everyone began to edge hopefully towards the lift.

Before they could disperse, however, there came the sound of several sharp handclaps and a harsh voice crying, 'If you please – attention!' A small, black-clothed woman, her head wrapped in a paisley turban which made her face seem larger and more yellow even than it was, made an imperious gesture. 'You – Partos Tours – come, come here to me!' she cried.

They came. She surveyed them with eyes narrow and glistening as black olives, set close on either side of a long camel's nose. She smiled, fearsomely. 'So. That is good. You come when I say. That is how it shall be, yes? From today till you leave Greece, yes? I call, you come. So.'

She regarded with satisfaction their stupefied faces. 'So. I know you but you don't know me, yes? I am Madame Aphrodite Mavrodopoulos and I am your guide. From now until you leave my country I tell you everything, take you everywhere, yes? You don't do one thing without I tell you except when you have special free time for visit shops, buy beautiful things. I tell you where. So. Soon I know all your names. Very quickly I learn all about you. And you learn all about me, yes? My name difficult for English people so you call me Madame Aphrodite, yes? You learn too that when I say Come, you come, quick, quick. If naughty boys and girls don't come when I say, they get left behind, yes?'

She smiled wolfishly, looking round the circle of faces and giving a little nod. 'So. Now to your rooms and then dinner, then as you please. But tomorrow . . .' She raised a terrible sun-baked hand. 'Tomorrow down here, all, at nine o'clock, yes? Not nine one minute, nine five minutes, but nine exact. Otherwise you get left behind. Tomorrow nine o'clock here for visit Acropolis, Philopappas, Agora. Return hotel, one o'clock lunch and siesta. Four o'clock exact, coach for Daphne, Eleusis and Piraeus. Next day we start on tour. Eight o'clock exact leave for Peloponnesus. So. Small luggage, yes? No forgettings. Ten days before we get back here. Now we say night-night until tomorrow. Nine o'clock exact and no silly shoes, please, or you break your legs. So. Sweet dreams.' She turned, an immense black handbag knocking at her bony hip, and spun through the revolving doors.

The coach party looked at each other. 'Ware minefields,' muttered the Major.

In another time and place Madame Aphrodite could have been a galley-master, standing astride the gangway on either side of which, day after sweltering day, her captives cringed in their allotted places. Over their bent heads her gaze swept like a lash, checking, identifying, while instead of the time-giver's drum her voice rasped out over the microphone a ceaseless flow of instruction.

For Madame Aphrodite (Madame Aspro, the Major called her after the second day, but not in her hearing) was extremely efficient. Not only did even hotel receptionists bend before her but she absolutely knew her Classical stuff. The glory of being Greek had consumed her, shrivelled her up, so that now, in old age (and who knew how old she could be, any more than Medusa, clambering up and down the slippery paving-stones, the ancient scree, an umbrella over her turbaned head, her yellow face dry as a lizard's while all those behind her sweated, sweated), it no longer illumined her with the rich, life-enhancing glow of an eternal flame but had seared her into a bitter, knotty brand which smoked and sparked and made the eyes water.

She knew everything, everything; and behind the facts she knew the spirit, the truth that had spread and fertilised and made the world beautiful so that always, for ever, mankind was in its debts. She knew the absolute truth, and the truth was herself; yet day after day from April to October, in her old age (how old, Medusa?), if she were lucky and resourceful, she must lay this truth out before coachloads of insensitive non-Greeks, must tell them facts and get them fed, make toilet stops and stops to buy souvenirs, must count them in and out of this shrine of majesty and that, see their eyes glaze at pillars, cloisters, Pantocrators, hear them whisper of heat or their bowels or the moussaka at that last place while she poured out on them the splendour of the Mysteries or of Marathon. The fury and frustration made her voice harsh and her eyes hard as she drove them sheep-like to and fro, telling them things they did not hear, showing them things they would not see. She knew everything, everything, and all they wanted were schoolroom facts and what time they'd be stopping for lunch.

She had a certain inbred respect for men, so the married couples and the three bachelors were more or less safe from her, although the lissome youngish man fared badly once or twice. But with the unattached women she was pitiless. Sarcastic comments about beauty sleep were made if they were late for the morning departures; and if they strayed from the main party during the day 'You have a boyfriend in the olive grove, yes? No use to look for the chauffeur, he has a wife and five children.' They smiled weakly and pretended it was a joke.

But the worst butt of all was that Miss Fordyce who had mislaid her tartan holdall on arrival in Omonia Square. Not only was Miss Fordyce magnetic to ill fortune but she contributed to it herself. That it should be her room that was over the kitchens or her washbasin which regurgitated someone else's scummy water was

140

bad luck, but that she should leave her cardigan in the arena at the very top of the ruins at Delphi or drop her sunglasses down the granite terraces of Epidaurus was her own fault. She should have known better than to eat that extremely greasy goat meat on the way to Olympia, certainly better than to insist that she was secure for the excursion next morning.

It was she who got lost in Nauplia (how can one lose one's way in Nauplia, for heaven's sake?) and who fell into a small crevasse at Corinth, spraining a wrist. Everyone agreed that Miss Fordyce was very game; and everyone wished that she were not in their party.

As the Major said, there is one on every trip, but with any luck they may be pretty or young or amusing and so their sins are forgiven them most of the time. Miss Fordyce was none of these things, but a big, lumpy, elderly woman with weak ankles, the result of a childhood illness that had nearly carried her off, as she told everyone several times, especially when her slowness in getting in or out of anything held up everyone else. 'Miss Fordyce, please to wait till the last so we don't lose too much time, yes? . . . Miss Fordyce, please to go to the coach now so we don't get waiting . . . Miss Fordyce, so often I tell you hold your feet in so we don't all fall over them, yes?' The nagging was incessant, and everyone else looked out of the windows or fussed with hand luggage.

As the most noticeably masculine man among them (for somehow marriage seemed to neutralise the husbands of the couples) the Major carried a certain weight, and Madame Aphrodite treated him with a fearsome archness. 'Ah, Major, come come come! Be so kind as to order the coffees while I see that the WCs are not locked.'

'Wilco,' would answer the Major, deftly steering Mrs Lambert to the most comfortable seat, then making sure they both got the first service.

Sometimes Madame Aphrodite sat at their table, watching derisively as they emptied the powdered coffee into their cups, her long nose inhaling the aroma of her own Greek brew (Greek,

141

not Turkish, yes?). Mrs Lambert sat very composedly on these occasions, knowing that Madame Aphrodite's glittering speculation was upon her, wondering what and why. She of all people knew how far apart at every hotel were Mrs Lambert's room and that of the Major.

The Major handled these coffee breaks with nervous gallantry, his face redder than ever, his blue eyes uneasy, a small boy at tea with Matron. Mrs Lambert admired him; she knew he was frightened of Madame Aphrodite, as were they all – except, probably, herself. As she had never, since she was a girl, felt herself inferior to anyone, Mrs Lambert had no reason to fear anything. But she was glad that the presence of the Major shielded her from Madame Aphrodite's lash.

Miss Fordyce, flopping and gasping under it, turned hither and thither for help. Sometimes she was allowed to take cover with a couple, married or female; but not for long because, ignoble though everyone knew it to be, they none of them wanted to be bothered with the poor creature. She was a bore; and, just as Madame Aphrodite implied, she was also a nuisance, delaying, irritating, trailing behind.

She turned to the Major; and he, kind-hearted and in some ways naive as he was, treated her gently. He listened to the story of her childhood illness; of her father who had been a noted archaeologist, which was why she had come to Greece; of her two cats and their quaint ways; of the literary circle of which she was the secretary, and the humdrum subjects of their meetings. She told him about the bad rooms, the bad food, the bad seats, the bad manners which, quite correctly, she felt she received wherever she went. But she did not dare to complain about Madame Aphrodite. Her fear and shame were too great.

The Major listened, sometimes humming under his breath. His gaze would wander to Mrs Lambert and they would exchange a small, smiling look. He had not much idea of how to extricate himself from Miss Fordyce, beyond looking at his watch and exclaiming, 'I say, just look at the time!' or, if he saw her approaching soon enough, turning his back and moving Mrs

Lambert hastily away, as though they had not noticed her. Soon Mrs Lambert began to abet him in this. She was sorry for Miss Fordyce for, before she met the Major, she had herself suffered many of the penalties of a middle-aged woman travelling alone. But she had never been so incompetent, so tiresome as Miss Fordyce. Besides, it was she who had the Major.

As they sat in their accustomed places in the coach Mrs Lambert thought seriously about the Major. The tour was almost over; they were on their way back to Athens, where tomorrow they would spend the morning shopping and, when the heat of the day subsided, visit Sounion to watch the sunset from the temple of Poseidon on the cliff. The next day back to England. And then what?

For Mrs Lambert knew that things could not remain exactly as they had been. You cannot, no matter how it seems, both have your cake and eat it. She had had the cake for six years; had the time come when she should eat it? His wistful looks, the occasional kissed hand, had all been signals that a slow swell was mounting. During the past ten days he had been noticeably tender; beyond the normal call of good manners he had cherished her in numberless little ways. The last few evenings, as the coach had neared its overnight stop, or after dinner, walking in the soft air beside the café tables, he had taken her hand and she had let him. Not during the daytime when anyone could see, but in the darkness of the coach or among the dusty oleanders of a little square. He had breathed heavily but said nothing; he did not dare, for although he had her hand she gave no sign that she was aware of it. Her gaze remained friendly but cool as it had always been, her voice calm. Thus she was when checking her income-tax assessment or acquiring a new property.

But Mrs Lambert knew that soon she must make up her mind. She did not actually want to, but as a business-woman she recognised that there is a time to buy and a time to sell, a time to make an offer and to receive one. By the time they returned to England she would have decided whether to marry the Major.

They saw the tiny ivory bones of the temple, standing high between the cobalt sky and the turquoise sea, long before they reached it. The heat of the day was declining and this, the last expedition of the tour, had an end-of-term air about it. This time tomorrow they would all be back at home again, reading the accumulated mail, watering the plants, drinking a decent cup of tea. They had enjoyed it all, of course; and the colour films which they would finish up now at Sounion would be despatched to the developers' first thing. But, as their coach drew in beside the others already parked there, they gathered themselves together more sluggishly, followed more slowly up the steep slope on which, still and golden against the cooling sky, the pillars awaited them; and heard with equanimity, for it was the last time, the leather-palmed clap-clap-clap, the leather-throated Come-come-come as Madame Aphrodite clambered on to a broken pediment and forced their attention.

For her too it was the end of term and she could hardly endure them a moment longer. Their lethargic assemblage, their wandering looks infuriated her and only by the exercise of greatest self-discipline could she summon them under her in their proper obedient knot to assert her own harsh commentary against the rivalling French and German groups who, with their own shrill guides, already milled and wallowed over the sacred stones.

'Come come come! Partos people, please to come here. Please to keep close for listening. Never mind looking now, now you listen, yes? Come come come!' She could hardly wait to be done with them, to deliver this last harangue into their bovine faces, to let them clamber about and take their silly snapshots and then shoo them back down the hill, into the coach, back to the city and out out out into oblivion, never to be seen again. She would accept their tips, crushing the notes into her big black handbag to count when she reached the haven of her own two rooms in a peeling house behind the University. Gnarled feet bare on the tiled floor, she would push open the shutters that had kept out the heat all day and breathe in the solitude, the peace of the tour's end. She would forget these Partos people utterly, expunge them, folding their tips into the old cashbox against her older age. Deny that, next Monday evening, there would be another lot to start with all over again.

Raising her voice, she crammed the final dose of information into their inattentive ears. Above the babel of the rival groups the columns breathed silence, the luminous sky darkening into the sea, the sun sliding down towards the headland where soon lights would come on and a new round of life begin in the seaside suburbs of the city. Far below the cliff where they swarmed at the foot of the temple two fishing boats passed like feathers across the rippled sea, and suddenly Madame Aphrodite could do no more.

'So. That is enough, yes? Now you must look for yourselves. Ten minutes only, then back quick quick to the coach. No waiting. Ten minutes only.' She climbed down and, turning her back on her party, pushed through the other groups and out of sight.

'Well,' said the Major, 'she cut that jolly short.' He took Mrs Lambert's elbow and helped her across the broken pavements to the cliff's edge and the sunset. 'Can't say I'll be sorry to see the last of the old girl. Bit of a battle-axe, eh? Still, knows her stuff.'

They stood and looked at the sunset, moving aside so as not to occlude the view of various photographers jockeying for space and angles. Two huge Germans crashed past them. His grip on her arm tightened. 'Wine-dark sea, eh? Can never quite see it, myself. But beautiful, beautiful. Something we'll never forget. I never will, anyway. Treasured memory – like so many, eh? Hilda . . .'

She moved away. Not here, with German and French and American clamorous about them, the scrape of feet, the click of cameras. She climbed up on to the temple floor and he hurried after her. 'Here, let me give you a hand.'

'Thank you.'

A large form swooped and clutched. 'Oh, Mrs Lambert, Major – do come! I've found it! I knew it was here because Father always maintained it was a fake. It wasn't at all his period, of course, but

145

to me it has always been an ambition, to actually see . . . Do come.'
Miss Fordyce, flushed, her cardigan slipping off her shoulders as
usual, drew them with her to the landward side of the temple,
stumbling over the pavings to one of the grooved columns. 'There
– see? It really is! Think of it, imagine it! Him standing there,
frowning perhaps, his hair blowing, carving away . . . What a thing
to do! Vandalism, of course, but still . . . There it is!' She reached
forward and let her fingers trace the letters carved into the stone.
'Byron!'

'Byron?'

'Lord Byron. She should have told us, for you'd easily miss it
if you didn't know it was here. Imagine!' Her face was radiant,
grey hair falling into her eyes. 'Do look. Do you see it?'

Mrs Lambert and the Major moved forward and Miss Fordyce
stepped back. Her foot slid and she fell awkwardly with a small
shriek. Several people nearby turned their heads but the Major
was bending over her.

'Oh dear,' she gasped. 'Oh dear. How silly of me.'

'Are you hurt?'

'No. No, I don't think so.' They helped her to her feet. 'Oh
dear. Wicked Lord Byron!' She smiled but her face was pale. Mrs
Lambert picked up her cardigan and put it round her.

'Oh dear, what a silly thing! I think perhaps I'll go back to the
coach. These places are dreadfully dangerous, really they ought
to warn you.'

'Let me help you.' The Major took her arm.

'Well, thank you – just down the hill. These stones, so
treacherous. But we did see Byron . . .'

Mrs Lambert watched them make their cautious way down the
eroded hillside and disappear between the ranked bodies of the
charabancs, pale now in the falling dusk. Some of the other
groups had already left but a number of people still crawled about
the temple, destroying the evening peace, and Mrs Lambert
wondered what it would be like to see it alone and silent, whether
the ghosts of those who had worshipped here would steal out, as
the stored heat did, from the stones. She let her fingers move as

Miss Fordyce's had over the flowing letters incised in the column, arrogant and elegant; Byron. She never read poetry, but just the same . . .

The Major had returned. 'Poor old thing – it would be her it happened to, eh?'

'Is she all right?'

'Perfectly. The coach was locked, no sign of the driver chappie, so I sat her down on the grass beside it and told her to wait. Madame Aspro'll be after us all in a moment anyway.'

Sure enough, soon they heard the clap clap clap of Madame Aphrodite, emerging from some hidden crevice of the cliff, and joined the others moving down the hillside to the parking-place. Madame Aphrodite came behind them, a testy sheepdog. It was almost dark now, suddenly. The driver was in his seat, the coach already pulsating. Everyone clambered in quickly, eager now for it all to be over. Madame Aphrodite climbed in last, surveyed them neatly packed in their double seats, counting under her breath.

Her face froze. 'There is one missing,' she grated. 'Who, please, is missing?'

A hush fell. Each looked guiltily at his neighbour, thanking God they were in their place. The driver revved the engine.

'Who, please, is missing?' Her voice was like a saw.

A whispered hiss went round the seats: Fordyce, Miss Fordyce, Fordyce . . .

'So. Miss Fordyce.' Madame Aphrodite folded her arms in menacing satisfaction. 'Always Miss Fordyce. Someone has seen Miss Fordyce, yes?' No one spoke. 'Miss Fordyce has perhaps fallen from the cliff? She has taken a taxi home? We are already ten minutes late and Andros here is needing his supper. Who knows of Miss Fordyce?'

Not a sound.

Mrs Lambert turned and looked at the Major. His face was flushed and he was staring at the back of the seat in front of him.

The driver let out a long blare on his klaxon.

Madame Aphrodite's yellow face grew pale. Her eyes seemed

to send out sparks of fury and she banged her handbag down on the hard little folding seat on which she had to travel.

'One more minute only we wait! Who has seen Miss Fordyce?'

The Major got to his feet. 'I'll go and look for her,' he muttered. The driver issued another terrible blast from his horn and revved the engine even more.

At the Major's movement everyone began to chatter: Just like her, always the same, silly old fool, lack of consideration, dead tired, want to get back and rest, some people never learn . . .

He bumbled his way down the aisle, Madame Aphrodite a knot of fury by the door. 'Shan't be a tick,' he said, and began to dismount; but as he did so a pale figure loomed out of the dusk and Miss Fordyce, distraught, staggered to the steps.

'Oh, thank goodness, thank goodness! I was afraid you'd have gone . . .'

The Major drew back. Miss Fordyce was literally wringing her hands, her hair on end, her voice a wail. 'So sorry but not my fault, not my fault at all. It was the wrong bus. I was waiting by the wrong bus.'

As she began to haul herself aboard the Major turned and retreated down the aisle. He looked neither to left nor right.

Madame Aphrodite's voice cut like a saw. 'So. The wrong bus.'

'Yes, quite the wrong bus. It was locked, you see, so I didn't notice, I just waited there . . .'

'You didn't notice. In ten days you don't notice the colour of the coach. You don't notice the name Partos written big, big on the sides? Do you notice more perhaps the colour of the driver's eyes?'

Miss Fordyce stood in the doorway staring in terror at Madame Aphrodite, whose small frame seemed to vibrate.

'You don't hear me say ten minutes only, you don't see us return down the path, you don't see us get in the coach marked Partos? You don't stay with everyone as I tell you always? You are dreaming perhaps of a rendezvous with Poseidon? You are a sea nymph, yes?'

148

'Oh!' Miss Fordyce went white, then a mottled raspberry. 'How dare you . . .'

'Get to your seat and let us have no more silly argument!' Madame Aphrodite snatched up her handbag from the hard little seat and plumped herself down in it, snarling over her shoulder, 'There is always one who is trouble to all the rest. I thank God my hands are now washed of you.'

Miss Fordyce stumbled to her seat, past the prim knees of the widower who had got landed with her at the beginning of the tour and who now clicked his knuckles nervously and stared straight ahead. With a lurch and a roar the coach began to move and was soon hastening, at well over the normal speed, back towards Athens.

It was quite dark now. On the one side lay the hills with their low trees and the villas of diplomats and rich Athenians pale among their greenery; on the other the sea, silent and calm as the night, lapping secretly along the shore. Sooner than seemed possible they reached the wide new road through the suburbs, edged by cafés and hotels, brightly lit and loud with music and traffic. Then away from the sea, back up the airport high-way, past the dry earth and desiccated buildings, back into the narrow turmoil, the heat, the lights, the crowded streets and cafés and, glimpsed now and then floating high above the roofs against the night sky, the tiny floodlit stillness of the Parthenon.

They reached the hotel. They gathered their belongings, edged down the aisle, climbed out. No one had spoken during the whole journey back, and even now they could not. Madame Aphrodite stood on the pavement, hunched and silent. Not looking at her, they shook her gnarled hand with mumbled thanks, leaving within it the notes on which they had decided earlier in the day. Silently she stuffed them into her bag, her long-nosed face impassive, her eyes remote. Only Miss Fordyce, tear-blotched and dishevelled, did not pause beside her but hurried past into the hotel and up into her room (next to the service lift), not to be seen again until next morning in the airport bus. She sat alone and spoke to no one, all the way back to Cromwell Road. And perhaps beyond.

The Major and Mrs Lambert spoke. At dinner they spoke about the menu, about the menus over the past ten days, about the places they had stayed and the objects they had bought; and they shared their conversation with several other members of the party, comparing notes and being promised copies of the photographs which all hoped would turn out satisfactory. Mrs Lambert excused herself from the Major's suggestion of a last turn together in Syntagma Square and went up to her room. Like Miss Fordyce, she did not appear until the airport bus was due; when the Major tapped on her door to see why she was not at breakfast she answered, without opening it, that a tray had been sent up and that she had not finished packing.

She let him queue for her at the Duty Free shop, and accepted quietly the bottle of perfume he bought her as a gift. She did not speak much on the flight but closed her eyes and kept her hands in her lap.

He retrieved their suitcases at Heathrow and carried them to the bus, paid their fares (nice to handle proper money again) and at Cromwell Road got a taxi.

She agreed that London looked dirty but that everything, as they neared Putney and his flat, looked nice and green; that it was good to be home again no matter what strikes and inflation might await them. When he fell silent, pursing his lips and glancing at her nervously out of the corners of his eyes, she said at last: 'How much did you tip Madame Aphrodite?'

'Madame Aspro?' He was alarmed. 'Haven't a clue, not now.'

'You must have some idea.' She opened her handbag and took out her purse.

'Oh – well, three hundred drachs, something like that. But really, I don't want . . . I mean, no need . . .'

She made a silent calculation, then put the right amount into his hand. He tried to give it back. 'Honestly, I don't want . . . That's always been my pigeon.'

150

'Please,' she said, her manner tranquil, 'I would rather take my share of Madame Aphrodite.'

He looked at her and she looked back. His round red face turned slowly redder still and he glanced away, fumbling the money into his pocket. 'Well, if you insist.'

'Yes,' she said.

They reached his block of flats and he got out. On the pavement he stood, his luggage beside him, bald head shining, gazing in.

'Hilda . . .' he said.

She leaned forward and swung the taxi door shut between them. 'Some other time,' she said.

The following year Mrs Lambert spent her holiday with her sister-in-law at Sidmouth. And the year after that.

She did not miss the Major.

Business lunch

Here we are. After you, old chap. It's a simple little place, nothing fancy, but they do a good bolognaise. Bon Giorno, Maria, comay sta? That's the extent of my knowledge of the lingo, I'm afraid. We'll have the corner table . . . Reserved? Ah. No, it's just the two. D'you mind being in the middle, old chap? It's a bit cramped, but . . . You're sure? Okay, then. They get very full at lunchtime, regulars, you know. I prefer a nice little place like this where they know you to one of those smart places where they charge the earth for nothing but a bit of show.

Grazie, Maria. Now, what'll you have?

A gin and tonic for my friend and I'll have a medium sherry – I have to keep off the hard stuff, the old insides, you know. And what'll you eat? Right. Two prawn cocktails, one escalope, and I'll have the rump steak and spaghetti. No, vegetables come with. And a carafe of the red? A carafe of the red, Maria. Great.

Well now, I've brought along the draft programme. It's only rough but you can take it it's pretty well the best procedure, stood the test of time, you know. We've followed it the last few years. Yes, these get-togethers were Bruce's baby, his idea – public relations, personal contacts and all that. But of course I do all the donkey work. It was my structure actually, basically, right from the start.

Well, the seminar proper kicks off with a reception on the Friday evening – informal, you know, short dresses for the ladies. Yes, in the Dolphin Room at the Grand. Most of them stay at the Grand but some of us prefer the Royal Victoria just round the corner. It's not as grand as the Grand, ha ha, but its more homely – and half the price, if one's got one's good lady with one, as I always do. Bruce always stayed at the Grand, of course, but his wife never came with him. And the Managing Director can always swing his expenses, can't he, ha ha.

Ah thanks, Maria. Cheers!

Well, after the reception we're what the Yanks call at leisure. Usually we make up small parties for a meal somewhere and some of the boys get together later for a bit of a booze-up. Bruce was a great one for that, always one of the boys, don't you know – must've had a head like iron for he was always bright-eyed and bushy-tailed first thing next morning. Booze-ups aren't my style, alas – the old insides, you know. And anyway, there's always a lot of preliminary work to do the night before, checking everything out, the programmes, timing, seating, mikes – these seminars don't run themselves, you know, and I can pretty well say there's no one knows more about running them than I do. Although, of course, it was always Bruce's show.

Ah thanks, Maria. Everything OK, old chap? Worcester sauce? Roll? We'll have the wine now, Maria.

The seminar starts sharp at 9.30 Saturday morning – yes, in the Dolphin Room again. I'll have checked it's all shipshape and Bristol fashion after the previous evening's shindig. You wouldn't believe the things that have to be checked – hotel staff are just no good these days, can't rely on any of them, foreigners who couldn't care less, even at posh places like the Grand. I tell my wife we get far better service round the corner where we are. Last year I found the platform wasn't even prepared – no carafes, no glasses, no ash trays, shocking. The year before that the schedules were late, I had to go round in a taxi and collect them from the printers. I tell you, it's a hell of a lot of hard work, running a seminar for a front man.

You've got the draft programme there? Fine. Well, the Managing Director kicks off, speaks for about fifteen minutes, welcomes everyone and all that. Outlines the theme for the seminar – we all know it, of course, The Impact of Sales Promotions on Sales Productivity. Then the Production Manager speaks. That takes us to eleven and the coffee break. Eleven thirty, the Sales

Manager speaks, then questions from the floor – that's you and your chappies, customers from all over – and break about twelve thirty. Buffet lunch, in the Old Tars' Tavern Room this time, one to two thirty. Two thirty, the Area Managers speak, each for ten minutes. Then the floor's open again for you and your colleagues. Fire in questions, anything you like. Six o'clock, Managing Director winds up.

Seven thirty, assemble in the Neptune Ballroom, black tie, and glad rags for the ladies, for the banquet and dinner-dance.

It's hard graft for yours truly, I can tell you, but rewarding, rewarding . . . One doesn't expect credit or any special thanks – that was never Bruce's way. But it's satisfying to know the job's been well done and everyone had a good time.

Ah thank you, Maria. Molto benie. Got everything you want, salt, pepper? Let me fill you up. No, I have to go slow, acid in the old insides. Well, bon appeteet.

Well, Sunday morning, strictly speaking, the seminar's over. I'm pretty well bushed by then, I can tell you. The whole responsibility for the smooth running of it all is on my shoulders right from the start. All behind the scenes, of course, it looks like Bruce's show from out front. I'm whacked by Sunday morning, but Bruce was a great one for informal get-togethers, small groups chatting ad hoc, bringing up points there hadn't been time for in the sessions, especially with individual customers like your goodself. There's a fair amount of drinking and I daresay the chats are useful, personal contacts, like you and me now, ha ha. Bruce would be breezing about in the bar doing his all-boys-together act – or sometimes he liked to hold court up in his room at the Grand, just one favoured person perhaps, tête-a-tête . . . He reckoned more business was done at his informal drinking and chatting meetings than at the whole of the seminar. Naturally I don't agree. Couldn't expect me to, could you ha ha, since the whole shebang was on the road entirely due to yours truly, old muggins here. Still, I never argued. One didn't argue with Bruce.

Yes, it was sad. Tragic. It shook us all, I can tell you. The prime of life, hardly that really, only forty-nine. Tragic. I'm sorry for his wife. Yes, two children. A great loss.

You never met him, did you? No, that's right, you took up the contract four, five months ago and Bruce went – what, well, a year ago, almost to the week, the last seminar, of course. Who should remember it better than me? Extraordinary chap he was. Dynamic. What he said, went. Ride roughshod over anyone, yet everyone seemed to like him. Especially the ladies. You could see them eyeing each other at the dinner-dance to see who he took out on the floor most often. I used to pull my wife's leg about it. How far it went I wouldn't know. His wife never came with him, and those Sunday morning chats in his room weren't all for the customers, I can tell you. Charisma, I think they call it. He certainly believed in himself. That's the secret, eh? Believe in yourself and others will do likewise.

Mind you, he was brilliant. No denying that. He had drive. He knew exactly what he wanted and he saw that he got it, never mind what other people felt. There's no doubt he worked wonders for the Company, no doubt at all. A real go-getter. Brilliant.

No, he'd not had much business experience. Not like most of us in the firm. Take me, for instance. I went into it almost straight from school, junior clerk, worked my way up. There's no one knows the Company better than I do, every aspect of it – stands to reason, after all these years. I could run any department you care to name, inside out I know it. I didn't do National Service, my old insides, you know. I just went into the Company and slogged my way up like none of the young ones bother to do nowadays. Always after new jobs, new experiences. Where will they be when they're sixty, I ask myself? On Social Security, you mark my words . . .

Take Bruce, for instance. Typical. Did his National Service in the Parachute Regiment and stayed on. Got to Major, served all over the place, saw plenty of action here and there. Must have enjoyed that. Came out, did a course in Business Studies – I ask you, Business Studies! – and straightaway got offered a plum job by the Company. Personnel he was at first – had the knack of handling men, we were told. Then up to Sales Manager. Then

Managing Director. Up like a rocket, without no experience at all. And down like a rocket too, of course. Tragic.

Now, what'll you have for afters? Nothing? You're sure? Ice cream, cheese? They do a good gâteau. Well, if you're sure. Just coffee, Maria – black for my friend, white for me. Grazie.

Yes, I was with him. He had this habit of having people up in his room on the Sunday morning. They'd be the favoured few, special customers he was out to catch. And, between you and me, women. I've a shrewd suspicion he had lady friends up there for a quiet session before getting into his Jaguar and heading home to his wife. A dynamic fellow, our Bruce.

Thanks, Maria. Sugar? A liqueur? Sure?

Yes, I was with him. It was just before lunch and me and the wife were just getting ready to leave for home. I'd been run off my feet all morning, paying bills, keeping contacts, tidying up all round after everyone while my wife took herself off for a walk along the front. I seldom have time to spend with my wife at these seminars, I'm at everyone's beck and call and she has to find her own amusements, I tell her. She's good at that. So she'd been out on her own and just got back and we'd got our bags packed, and just when I thought I was off the hook a summons comes from his lordship to go up to his room.

He had this habit of summoning one to his room and tearing a strip off one. That's if he hadn't got better fish to fry, of course. He'd want to go over the whole thing, query and criticise, that sort of thing. Things that could perfectly well have waited to sort out in the office next morning, but well, that was Bruce's way. Like being sent for by the headmaster. One didn't argue.

The chambermaid hadn't been in yet. The room was a mess, suitcase open, the bed all tumbled, ashtrays stinking, and a couple of glasses and a bottle on the bedside table. The room was one of the best, naturally, on the top floor with a lovely view of the sea. Bruce was standing in the french windows, they were open on to the little balcony, more like a windowsill really with just a low rail, and the net curtains were blowing to and fro round him. He was in his shirtsleeves and had a drink in his hand. I could tell he'd had a few by his voice, and he was sort of flushed and bright-eyed – you know, like he'd just had a good workout or something to set him up. He had this rough way of speaking to you, never gave you time to answer, as though he was back in the guardroom or somewhere and this was a court martial. He'd just fire questions and criticisms at you, 'No excuses!' if you opened your mouth. The room was a pigsty, all those bedclothes tumbled about and the ashtrays and the smell of stale smoke and drink, and that small snap-purse women keep their make-up in in their handbags lying there on the floor by the bed, just like my wife's got . . .

More coffee? Sure?

Well, he started the usual criticisms about the way the seminar had gone, with his back half turned to me and the glass in his hand. Didn't even look at me, just stood there criticising. And then – well, I simply don't know what happened. It must have been some kind of heart attack – although the inquest brought in Misadventure. My own view is that he was drunker than I thought and just blacked out. Anyway, as we all know, he fell over the balcony – twelve storeys down and crashed through the hotel canopy. My God, it was frightful! I saw him go and just couldn't do a thing to stop him – I rushed over and tried to catch hold of him but he'd gone . . . I'll never forget it. I stood there in that pigsty of a room and thought. 'He's gone. Bruce is gone.'

Well, these things happen. Life goes on. But what a tragedy, eh? A brilliant chap, charismatic. Put the Company on its feet, no doubt of that. Mind you, it was always a real going concern, as I'm sure you fully appreciate. This seminar next week will show you just how effective we are as a team that can supply just the kind of commodity you're looking for. Bruce's sad passing won't affect that. So me and my wife look forward to seeing you there and we'll do our best to see you have a really worthwhile experience.

La conto, Maria, please. Grazie molto. I'll just give you our latest brochures. And the programme for the seminar. Any queries you have, don't hesitate to give me a buzz. Or any problems with the hotel – the Grand? Should be OK. We're round the corner, of course, as usual. Most of the guests will be at the Grand but we find the Victoria more homely. Tommy Mulgrave, Mr Mulgrave, our new Managing Director, he's at the Grand, of course. Yes, he was appointed last month. Quite a surprise. We'd thought perhaps the Board would promote some-one from inside the Company, someone who knows it all inside out . . . But they say he's a brilliant chap, in his mid-forties. Been in advertising somewhere, open up new horizons and all that. I'm still in charge of the seminar, naturally. Yes, I'm still plugging away, like always. I know the ropes, you see, inside out. It could none of it happen but for old muggins here.

What became of the purse? What purse? You must've misheard me, old chap. There was nothing found in the room that didn't belong to Bruce himself, poor fellow. I'll always remember that room and the curtains blowing and the way he just pitched over the rail . . .

Thank you, Maria. A riverderchi. After you, old chap.

*

A day like any other

*

My name is Winifred May Winter, of 13, Upper Lane, Halecot, Warwickshire. My age is fifty-one or fifty-two, I'm not sure which, but I was married in 1910 and Kenneth was born two years later, and he's thirty-two next March, so it's near enough for you, I hope. If not, I can easily look it up in Granddad's Bible. It's all there, and Kenneth's and Maureen's birth-dates, too, and Dad's and everything . . .

Oh, dear! I'm sorry. I'm doing my best to keep hold. I keep telling myself this is just an ordinary day like any other, but then it comes over me again. There. I'm sorry. I'll try and remember everything for you if you'll just let me tell it in my own way.

Well, this morning I got up at seven and went to church, like I always do when Dad's away. When the children were at home, of course, I never could, what with their breakfast and getting them off to school or work when they were older; and then when Dad's home I like to bring him his tea in bed and be with him while he reads the papers, and so on. He's a newspaper traveller, on the circulation staff of the Daily Post . . . Oh, but of course, you know that, don't you? I was forgetting . . .

Well, it was one of our little jokes to read the papers together when he's home at the week-end, and, just for fun-like, sometimes I used to make out I liked the others better than the Post, and I'd read out that one of them had ever so much bigger a sale figure than the Post had, and he'd sit up sudden, quite serious, and grab it out of my hand and say: 'Where? They can't have pulled ahead like that,' and then he'd see I was having him on, and we'd have a good laugh together . . .

Oh, dear! I'm sorry.

Well, this morning, as I was saying, I went to church, like I always do when Dad's not home, because I like to start the day with a bit of prayer for all of us – what with Kenneth in the Navy and Maureen a nurse and Dad away all the week. Of course, they're never absent from my thoughts for very long at any time, but in church you somehow feel your prayers get through to your loved ones more, as though they could really hear you . . .

Well, when I came back Mrs. Grinstead was here already. She'd got the boiler going nicely, but she'd broken a cup. It was Dad's special cup that he always has his breakfast tea in, and I was very upset about it. It had been cracked a long time, of course, but I can't help feeling she'd been careless with it, and I had warned her, knowing what store he set by it. He loves his home, Dad does. He's sometimes said to me: 'I come home to a home that *is* a home – all my own bits and pieces just as I like them, and my own old girl too . . .'

No, thank you. I'm quite all right really. Just let me go on in my own way.

Well, I spoke to Mrs Grinstead rather sharp, and then I had my breakfast and read the papers. I keep all the papers for Dad to see at the week-end, and I mark all the bits that interest me special or I think will interest him. He says it helps him in his reports to know what interests the ordinary reader, you see, and I always took pride in being able to take part in his work even ever so little. Because I believe a wife ought to take pride in her hubby's work, as well as seeing he has the kind of home he likes. Then it's a real partnership. It must be, mustn't it?

Well, I remember I marked a piece about queues and a piece where it said about the war criminals being tried in Germany, and two pieces to add to our serial. That was another of our jokes. While he as away I used to choose something – a murder or a law case or something – and mark all the bits in the papers about it every day so's he could read it just like a serial when he came home. I'd got two this week – where a man and woman had been found dead in a car somewhere out Birmingham way, and where the Town Council of some seaside place was having a row about all their empty houses not being occupied. Dad always said that was a scandal. I used to point out that, after all, we had the two empty rooms the children used to have, but he always said that was different, because Kenny or Maureen might need them any time if they came home again, and of course I had to agree.

Well, I marked the papers and cut out the Food Flash – although, really, if one doesn't know how to eke out the sugar ration by now you don't deserve to get any – still, they are helpful mostly, of course – and then I gave the sitting-room a good turn out, because Mrs Grinstead only just flicks the dust about, and I like the place to look perfect when Dad gets home. He usually gets home during the afternoon of a Saturday – it varies, but it's always before supper-time. I can always count on that, you see, because he knows I get something special for him, and he wouldn't want it to spoil from waiting. That's why . . .

No. Let me go on like I am.

Well, then I went out to the shops, just for the final odds and ends, you know. I went to get Dad's beer, and Miss Walker in the off-licence said something about a giant refreshed, which I thought rather pert, and some chocolate biscuits, and Mr Buxton gave me a bone for Maxie as well as our half a leg. I save up the meat ration for when Dad's home; a big man like that needs good food, and all this starch isn't satisfying, you know.

Well, then I went into Kate's Kettle for a bite of lunch – just a salad and a cup of tea, on account of having dinner in the evening, it being Saturday, of course. I passed a few words with Mrs Mortlake – that's the doctor's wife – and the young woman who's been at the Coach and Horses since Easter, I think it must've been. She said something about was Mr Winter coming home to-day. I didn't pursue the subject with her, because she's not the type of girl I very much care for; not at all the sort for a small town, although they never do stay long, of course.

Well, then I came home and gave Dad's Sunday suit a good brush and his shoes, and saw that there was tobacco in his jar, and all those sort of things, you know. And then I put my feet up for half an hour, because I like to be fresh when he comes back. He always has so much to tell me – how the sales are keeping up and what feature seems to be selling the paper best, and what London Office has said, and all that. And then about four I put the kettle on, half-expecting he might be back in time, you know, although quite likely not. He never could be certain to the minute when he'd be back, you see, travelling about so much, so I didn't worry, but had my tea and read the evening paper when it came. And I remember reading some more about the couple in the car, and how, although the car'd all been sealed up and they'd been gassed, the doctor said there were marks on their heads like they'd been stunned first, and they hadn't any identity-cards, and I thought what a lot of trouble to go to. And there was more about the housewives protesting about the queues again, and the shopkeepers were hitting back at them about it, and a nice breach-of-promise case I was ever so pleased to see, because I always laugh at Dad on account of him liking something a bit what he calls spicy.

Well, time was getting on, and I put the joint in the oven and hoped Dad'd hurry up. Then I did a little bit of weeding in the garden, keeping one eye on the road for Dad, but I didn't do much, because it makes me too hot now I'm a bit stout, and I didn't want to look a sight.

Well, it got to seven o'clock and then eight, and the joint was spoiling. I began to get a bit anxious, because it's not like Dad to be as late as that, and anyway, he could always 'phone Mrs Parks next door and she'd bring me the message. Maxie was wanting his walk, so I had to take him just up and down the road, but I didn't go far; not out of sight of the gate, because of looking out for Dad.

Well, finally I went in to Mrs Parks's, when it was getting on for nine, just to make sure he'd not left a message and she'd forgotten. But she'd not heard a word, and she could see I was worried, so she made me sit down and have a cup of tea with her, but I couldn't fancy it. My ears were too much on the tip for Dad's car driving up.

Well, time went on and went on, and I didn't know what to do. I began to get frantic, and Mrs Parks rang up the hospital, just in case there'd been an accident. He'd never been so late before. He'd never given me the least cause for anxiety in all our married life. He was the ideal hubby for any woman. I couldn't ask for a better . . .

Oh, dear! Do I have to go on? You know it all from then on. It was nearly one in the morning when this other gentleman here called and told me. That there'd been an accident I was expecting by now. Dad'd never have left me not knowing like that. But that it was him, in the car . . . And that girl, for months . . . And you saying it's her husband who did it . . . And me reading it in the paper like that, and not knowing . . . not knowing at all . . .

A natural death

Sophie's affair with Charles Foster had come to an end just on a year ago. It had lasted for six years, rather to her (and perhaps his) surprise, for it had been based more on friendship, splendidly fortified by sex, than on love, which had suited her (and certainly him) very well. She did not intend ever again to love anyone as much as she had loved her husband, and when he had insisted she divorce him eleven years before (to marry a woman far less attractive but, he had said, with 'more intellectual depth') only the bringing up of their two children had given her some sort of discipline for keeping on. That was how it had seemed at the time.

But Sophie had been used to love. All her life someone had cherished her – parents, admirers, a lover or two, and then John. After a period of dejection after the divorce she had been revivified by a virile, rather vulgar Dane she met on holiday – a disaster really, but at least it had encouraged her to believe she was still capable of attracting. Then, after nearly a year, there was that photographer – too young and not firmly anchored sexually; and then Paul, who was intense during that Design conference in Frankfurt; and then Charles, who for some reason had lasted more than a week or a month, with whom she had exchanged laughter and gossip and pleasurable affection, who had no intention of leaving his wife just as Sophie had no intention of wishing him to do so. Since the divorce she had built up a career as Design Consultant for a glossy monthly. Among other well dressed, well tinted women of a certain age, she was one of the most sparkling and successful. She liked it that way. Charles liked it that way. For six pleasant years they had contributed to each other's well-being, no strings, no demands.

164

Then gradually, as the seventh year grew closer, the relationship began to fade. Gently, nothing positive, until one day Sophie realised it was several weeks since they had even telephoned each other. The affair had died a natural death.

Natural? Well yes, natural. Six years is a long time for something that's not important. And yet – could the demise have dated from that evening when, afterwards, they had gone out to dinner and over the coffee she'd had at last to say, 'I forgot to tell you – Lucinda's having a baby.'

'Really?' He wasn't much interested, having never met, or perhaps even visualised, her daughter Lucinda. Perhaps he had assumed she was still a child, although of course he knew she was married just as he knew Giles was working in Canada. Their children had never impinged on their relationship, which was solely between consenting, confident adults, a 'fun' thing. 'When?'

'December.' It was September then. 'It does seem fantastic.'

'Yes. Will you have a brandy?'

'Lovely.'

That was all. But was it from then that things began to dwindle? She couldn't have concealed Lucinda's condition for ever, blanked out from him altogether one important section of her life. Lucinda was, after all, her child, her darling if often baffling daughter, not a schoolgirl but twenty-eight years old, married to Anthony, living in Fulham, and expecting a baby in three months' time. No matter how she evaded it, the inescapable fact was that Sophie would be a grandmother.

When she said 'fantastic', that was exactly what she meant. This gay, not very profound, slender woman with hardly any lines, no pouches or sags, her hair skilfully cut and discreetly highlighted, who moved lithely and made love voluptuously, could not, surely, be a grandmother? Shawls, caps, knitting? Granny? Grandma? It was ridiculous.

But true.

At first Sophie had hardly had time to notice that Charles was no longer around. Too many things were happening. The last months of Lucinda's pregnancy had been anxious, all was not quite well, Anthony distracted; the weather foul; a strike disrupting the magazine's production with consequent cancellations and rearrangements of Sophie's design feature; Giles unexpectedly flying in from Toronto and camping in Sophie's flat; and then, prematurely, Lucinda's baby. Whipped into hospital, blood transfusions, Anthony white and trembling, cigarette after cigarette in the blank waiting room, surging terrors and memories – of John and another maternity ward, of Lucinda as a baby, a child, a girl, a bride, a disorganised, dreamy, loved young matron. And then the release, the calm; Lucinda radiant although depleted and Anthony radiant although looking as though he would faint, and in the aseptic, perspex-walled crib (more like a kitchen fitment in one of Sophie's designs than a nest for a baby) the baby. A boy. Sophie's grandson.

A little skinned rabbit, fast asleep, faintly yellow from jaundice, tightly swaddled on its sterilised mattress in its clinical cot. Its tiny, closed face and head John's. Exactly.

A gush of such primitive emotion flooded Sophie that she could only stand and stare. In her heart she snatched up the creature and rushed with it out of the hospital to some lair where, huddling it to her breast, she cowered and snarled at any who tried to enter.

In reality she stood and stared, smiling, and from a long way off heard herself saying mildly, 'How fantastic, darlings.'

That was nine months ago. Now Sophie found herself, of all improbable things, on holiday with Lucinda, Anthony and the baby, in a not very comfortable hotel in Cornwall. How on earth had this come about?

After the first emotional surge at Dominic's birth Sophie had rigorously lived her own life. She saw them all, of course. Lucinda, dreamy and still disorganised, her hair still hanging limply, her face still bare of make up, her body still unsupported within the trailing flounces that Sophie so deplored, sometimes brought the baby to visit in his carrycot; and of course Sophie went to Fulham quite often, taking bottles of Tio Pepe and jars of expensive face cream, neither of which ever seemed to be opened. But her approach to Dominic was cool, she held him as little as possible, refused to change nappies or sterilise teats or do anything whatsoever that would underline their relationship. She had bought a lot of new clothes, had her hair restyled, had herself massaged, oiled and creamed from top to toe once a month. On the magazine she had now been made Design Editor, with an assistant and an on-call photographer. She looked, and was, brilliant.

How, then, came she to be on a family holiday in Cornwall? Because she loved them, of course, but also because a planned jaunt to Stockholm to do a piece on Scandinavian glass for the magazine had fallen through. Lucinda had seemed to want her, London was empty of interest and Sophie was beginning to realise it. She missed not exactly Charles but *a* Charles.

So here she was.

She had travelled separately by train in a civilised manner; not for her the hugger-mugger of a day-long car journey with a baby, thanks very much. But entering the dining-room for breakfast the first morning, seeing the elderly couples, the one or two families with school-age children, Lucinda in a smock, Anthony's beard, Dominic spilling cereal on the hotel's high-chair, she felt she was mad. The grapefruit juice was tinned and tepid, the toast cold and leathery. You had to go to the village for newspapers. There was a high wind driving the grey waves up the shore. This time last year – no, the year before – she and Charles had been in Amalfi for the weekend, he extending a business trip, she playing hookey from a journalistic jaunt organised by an Italian ceramic company.

Two years ago. Two years older – never mind. If (as she had always insisted) she had been twenty when Giles was born, that made her only fifty now. Fifty. My mistress is fifty and a grand-mother. Heavens!

A steely determination began to fill her. She loved Lucinda, was fond of Anthony, but from the baby (who no longer re-sembled John) she resolutely withheld herself, even though the beaming innocence of his regard, the way his soft hair grew, the pure white of his eyeballs turned a deeply defended part of her to jelly. Smiling, gay, immaculately dressed in trouser suits of superb cut or, in the evening, long skirts of expensive material, even flirting a little with Anthony (who didn't notice), she tried to live her own holiday alongside rather than with the others, seeing herself as an alien, exotic visitant from a different, her own, sophisticated world. She had come with them out of affection; that was enough. Looking at herself in the mirror (awkwardly placed in the too-small bedroom outside which the seagulls sniggered all day) she felt that no one could possibly take her for a day over forty-five, Lucinda's stepmother perhaps, if not quite her elder sister. Soon she would be able to blank out that ghastly incident in the lounge one evening when Lucinda and Anthony had gone off to the pub and Sophie was sitting in with the new Dick Francis. One of the pair of elderly women, white-haired, thick hipped, in powder-blue crimplene and white shoes, had paused by her chair and said, 'Sitting in, are you? That's nice. They're lucky to have a granny with them, I'm sure.' She had frozen, a smile cold as a deep-freeze on her immaculate lips. 'Well, they're a comfort, grandchildren, that's what I always say.' The woman had moved on, leaving Dick Francis's pages a grey splodge before Sophie's reading-glasses. Fortunately the woman left the following day.

Fortunately, because who knows what other ghastly things she might have uttered in full hearing in the lounge, and especially because it so happened that later the same day a rather presentable man appeared. In his forties, perhaps, tall, hardly grey. Casually well dressed, drinking the best claret the hotel could offer (which wasn't much), smoking a cigar whose smell hung in the lounge after he had left it. A man alone – divorced, widowed, queer? Surely not queer – he had regarded her with some interest as she came in to dinner with Lucinda and Anthony, an elegant rose between two flounced or hairy thistles, and had held the door open for her with a smile when they met in the hall next morning. In the evening they had talked a little. 'I'm here with my daughter and son-in-law,' she said, over the execrable coffee (no mention of Dominic).

'Surely not?' he said, 'I congratulate you.'

No, surely not queer.

A little pulse of excitement began to stir. He would be gone in a day or two, of course, but he really was rather her kind of man. In a merchant bank, she gathered – he drove a steel-coloured Jensen. Dolphin Square – so probably no wife? He played bridge, which she did not; but knew all about the newest plays and appeared to have a box at the Festival Hall. Why no woman? Perhaps, like herself, he was between relationships . . .

Her fantasies began to be really rather absurd.

Anthony liked to drive about and sample various small bays each day if the weather were fine, as on the whole it was. Dominic strapped in his car seat, baskets of nappies, bathing things, orange juice, rusks and repulsive plastic toys at their feet, they all set off over the strange Cornish landscape, so barren one minute, so deeply lush the next. Sophie went with them because she loved them and because there was absolutely nothing to do if she did not – the grey Jensen had gone off before they had finished breakfast but would be back that evening. Sitting in the back seat beside Dominic she allowed her thoughts to anticipate a future which repeated Charles, allowing Dominic to examine and chew the various rings which enhanced her sleek fingers without really noticing. Only when he began to probe her ears did she stir from her day-dreams. A beaker of orange juice diverted him.

They found a bay, yellow-sanded and clawed at either end by rocks, and, laden with impedimenta, ploughed over the dry dunes from the car park to the harder beach below. A sharp wind greeted them but the sun was out, and they tramped across to the lee of the rocks (the best places taken already by earlier arrivals) and settled at last in not too bad a nook. Anthony stripped to his bathing trunks and ran to and fro beside the waves, beating his chest, his beard blowing back like spume. Then he plunged in and swam fiercely, returning quite grey with cold. Heavily sweatered, he demanded soup and the picnic began. Sand crunched in their teeth and Dominic refused not to crawl over the sandwiches. The thermos overtipped and there was no knife for the crisp apples into which only Sophie could not bite with confidence. She found tar on her favourite tan slacks, the sun went in, and the wind changed round to blow into their crevice.

'Darlings,' she said, 'I really think I'll go back to the car.' The wind whipped out from under her Jacqmar headscarf the long lock of hair which it was vital to keep in place if she were to look like anything at dinner that evening.

'Do you?' Lucinda, unmarred by the weather since there was nothing there to mar, wrestled with a yelling Dominic. 'I think the sun's coming out again soon.'

'Even so.' She got to her feet (she had to get gracefully round to her knees and push herself up rather than do it in one springing movement as Lucinda did). 'I'll have a little read.'

Dominic was managing to scream even though his thumb was in his mouth. Neighbouring children stood and stared. Lucinda said, 'Could you possibly take him with you? He's awfully tired and he'll never settle down here with so much going on.'

'Well . . .'

'Put him down on the rug on the back seat and he'll soon go off.' She looked wistfully at the sea, which was calming now that the wind had changed. 'I should so like to bathe.'

'Of course, darling.' She shifted her shoulderbag.

'Anthony'll take him for you – oh, he's asleep.' So he was or seemed to be, face down on the sandy rug, the pale soles of his feet flecked with tar.

'I can manage. Whoops!' She staggered as the baby was put into her arms.

'Are you sure?'

'Of course. I coped with you and Giles, didn't I?'

She set off up the beach, the bag slipping from her shoulder to bang at her knee, the wind lashing her hair across her eyes as the baby lashed about him with his small but surprisingly hard hands.

Ploughing and reeling through the dunes, she reached the car park (a bared space, patchily tarmacked, between heath and beach) and thankfully got both of them inside. The baby stopped yelling and seemed pleased, but when she spread out the rug and laid him on it, on his stomach as he preferred, he began to roar again, rearing up. There was nothing for it but to stay beside him and hold him down, patting him gently with her other hand and crooning 'Hush now, hush, hush you silly little baby, hush . . .' Gradually, angrily, he surrendered. With an occasional twitch and sob, he sank like a stone into sleep.

She removed her hands and folded them in her lap. Her book was in the dashboard compartment and she dared not move to get it in case she woke him. So she sat and looked out of the windows, at the other ranked cars and the yellowy grass of the heath, the gorse bushes, and beyond them the sand with its tar patches invisible, the frothy edging of the waves which lapped gently now, changed to turquoise and, further out, navy blue under a sun which sailed clear from the scudding clouds. Through the open windows came a constant susurration of sound – sea and wind and voices, dogs barking, the ubiquitous, gibbering gulls.

She sat. From time to time she glanced down at the baby by her side. He was flushed in sleep, his eyelashes seeming at least half an inch long over his cheeks, his thumb dropped out of his mouth but still wet and sucked looking. His chest rose and fell and when she laid her hand on him, pulling the blanket up a little, she could feel his heart beating, fiercely, like a small clock. She let her hand lie there and with the other untied the scarf and shook out her hair. This strong damp wind was hell. Thank God for lacquer . . .

She sat. Out in the waves sometimes she saw heads which might be Lucinda and Anthony, round seal heads, sleeked down with water which would dry out and be forgotten with no more than a towelling and a rough comb. The heads bobbed together, first one pulled under, then the other, then coming together in what must be a kiss, with wet young slithery bodies adrift against each other in the pulsing turquoise, then flinging apart and racing, racing . . .

171

She was pierced with longing, with memory. She too, she too, more than they ever would, long ago and not so long ago, shaded siestas and going out after in the cool of twilight, mornings half awake before the children were up, mad half-dressed moments, giggling and impromptu; the six o'clock, the bedtime, the quarter-hour before the alarm clock sounded . . . All that couldn't be over, laid away. She was Sophie, who had always been loved. Until a year ago there had been Charles, lasting all that time. There would be others. If not the Jensen man, then someone else. She was slender, elegant, amusing. She dressed well, talked well, made love well. She had so much to give and to be taken. What did years matter, what did they take away that was important? Which was the more desirable, herself or darling raw Lucinda?

And as she stared out of the window, feeling power and confidence rise strongly up in her like wine filling up a glass, her gaze focused on a girl. She had come out from somewhere behind them and now ran up along the edge of the heath on the harsh springy turf to stand for a moment on the crest, her back to the cars and Sophie, looking out to the sea.

She was to all intents naked, for only the string of her coral-coloured bikini crossed her shoulders, only a tiny triangle masked the cleft of her buttocks. She stood, one arm raised so that her hand could shade her eyes, her long fair hair flying sideways in the wind to expose the line of her cheek and the rounded neck. Her uplifted arm was slender, the long line from naked shoulder to waist to hip to long smooth legs melodious as a phrase of music. The moulding of her spine, deepening just above her buttocks, was as though drawn by a sensuous thumb, just as the small waist, blossoming out to the hips, might have been turned on some master potter's wheel. She was a figurine of gold and ivory and alabaster, shimmering against the now totally blue sky, the deeper sea, the green and yellow of gorse and dune, the taut warm wild wind.

For a moment or two she stood so, poised, scanning the shore. Then she was off, hair flying, sure-footed over the tussocks and debris of the dunes where the waves never washed, bending and balancing, sinuous as a fish, fearlessly out of sight.

It was as though the heavens had opened and Jove had hurled a thunderbolt. It homed straight in on Sophie.

She did not say much when Lucinda and Anthony came back to the car, moist and laughing, shedding sand over everything; nor as Dominic awoke and crawled about the seat and her; nor as they drove back to the hotel, the two chattering to each other in the exhilarated aftermath of physical joy. She said no more when they got back to the hotel and separated to their rooms.

In hers, she took off her slacks and sweater, hanging them carefully, her sandals, shaking the sand out of the window. In her pants and bra she put on her dressing-gown and lay down on the bed. A faint smell of the evening meal had already seeped into the room, and the light outside was mellowing. Car doors slammed, and the seagulls were starting their usual evening squall.

She lay for a long time, flat. At one point she raised one leg and stared at it. Blue veins were beginning to show and the shinbone stood out more than it had. The hairs on it would be wiry did she not depilate them regularly. The varnish on her toenails seemed crude.

She studied her hand and her arm where the sleeve fell away from it. There was flab under the upper arm, and on her forearm the muscles seemed to show more than they used, as though the flesh were receding. Her hands were still beautiful; but the skin had become a little too fine. And were those freckles or – she blenched but faced the terrible term – grave spots?

After a while she got up and drew the curtains. The smell of dinner was stronger, and she saw she would be late if she did not hurry. Nevertheless she redid her face and hair with the greatest attention, skilfully as the years had taught her; the beach wind had not quite ruined that lock of hair. She dressed with care, her dark blue jersey skirt, a cream silk shirt, a scarf knotted low. Perfume, a touch. Lacquer, a waft. Taking her handbag, she went downstairs.

Lucinda and Anthony had the ill-judged custom of keeping Dominic up until dinner was actually served. They liked to show him off to the gathered guests, for he was at his most attractive then, encased in his sleeping-suit, all pink and sweet-smelling from his bath, drowsy but benign. A little group of admirers stood around him where he nestled against Lucinda, thumb in mouth; but as Sophie approached he saw her and leaned outward towards her uttering his own sounds of welcome. Murmurs of appreciation went round the group.

Sophie came forward. Smiling, immaculate head erect, not even looking to see whether the Jensen man were there or not, she held out her arms and said, 'That's lovely, darling – come to Granny.'

Coming south

*

Fancy me just happening to see it in the newspaper! Right down at the bottom of an inside page it was, only a few lines, I could easy have missed it. DEATH IN PRISON, it said, and underneath: 'Frank Wisbey, sentenced to life imprisonment in 1961 for the murder of his wife Edna, has died in Hackenfield Prison. He was fifty-eight.'

It gave me a turn, I can tell you. After all these years. Death comes to us all, of course; and of course, if it hadn't been for them changing the law Frank Wisbey would have been hung. Still, no matter what they found him guilty of, one wouldn't want that, would one, it's not nice to think about.

Well, when I read that piece in the evening newspaper I had to sit down. My legs just gave way. After a bit I got up and made myself a cup of tea, and as I sat and drank it of course I knew what I had to do. I'd always known, of course. But somehow it made me feel ever so funny. Ever such a funny mixture, I felt.

So the next morning I said to Mr Harding I had to have a few days off on account of urgent business. He didn't like it much and grumbled a bit but in the end he had to agree. I'm the best typing pool supervisor he's ever had and he knows it. I can keep those silly young girls in order like nobody's business, some of them have been there nearly six months and their work's as good as you'll find anywhere. I have my standards and I see they keep to them. They're only bits of girls, they respect authority if it's done with a smile. And I always smile. Whatever I feel inside, seething I may be, but I keep a smile.

So in my lunch hour I went to the travel agent and got my ticket to London for the next day. Tell you the truth, I quite looked forward to it. I hadn't been south for – oh, donkey's years and one can always do with a bit of a break, specially when you're as conscientious a worker as I am, and frankly, there's lots of places I'd rather live than what they call the industrial north. But I will say this for them, there's plenty of Go in them up there and they mind their own business. On the whole I've not regretted it. I've a good position and a nice little flat a bit outside the city, right on the bus route. I keep it like a new pin, I can tell you, and I've lived very comfortable there these last few years, with no one to mess the place up and upset me or interfere. That's why I came in the first place.

Well, I packed a case and gave the flat a good clean (not that it needed it, but I like to have everything nice) and next morning I got on the train for London. I was nervous, I don't mind admitting it. But I've never let nerves stand in the way of what I've determined to do.

It's not that I'm nervous of travelling, I've got more sense than that. Though I've not been abroad like everyone else these days, I've been to Scotland on a coach trip and I even flew to Ireland on holiday one year – before the Troubles, of course – and I wasn't a bit nervous in the plane. You see those silly bits of stewardesses that do it all the time, with their fancy hair-does and false eyelashes and nail varnish, and if they're not nervous it's not likely I'll be! No, I was nervous of going back. Yes I was, I was nervous.

Well, I needn't have been, of course. Not many people travelling, business gentlemen mostly, it being mid-week, and quite a nice clean train. I treated myself to a meal in the dining-car and it wasn't near so bad as what people make out. Quite nice really, and wonderful how those waiters don't spill anything. I closed my eyes for forty winks afterwards and it was dark by the time we got to London – and on time too. The railways aren't half so black as they're painted, if you ask me.

Anyway, I got a bus from the terminus (my word, how it's changed since I was there last!) and I found myself a room in a nice clean little hotel not far away and I took off my hat and coat and shoes and lay down on the bed, and here I am, going over it all in my mind. Until now, you see, I've just sort of acted automatic. After seeing that piece in the newspaper and getting over the shock, I'd known what I had to do, I made my plans and carried them through, just like I always do. But now, with nothing more to be done till tomorrow, I find it's all going round and round in my mind, over and over, just like I was reading it all in the newspaper again like it all came out at the trial, eleven years ago.

Frank Wisbey worked in the Accounts department of one of them big factories out to the south of London, the real country not all that far away by car for a nice run at the weekend, and one of them big sewage farms, they call them, quite nearby, which wasn't all that nice really, I suppose, but you wouldn't notice it. He and his wife had a nice little house of their own, built in the 1920s, semi-detached, a nice bit of garden front and back. But what made it really nice was the back-garden ran down to a foot-path along all the backs of the gardens and came out on a recreation ground, so it could never be built on. Cricket and football, a playground for the kiddies, a pond and a dirty old stream that fed it, more like a ditch really. But it was a really nice place to live and you'd never believe you was only a stone's throw away from the motorway – you know the kind of place.

They didn't have any children. She kept the house nice and he did the garden and they was as decent, respectable a couple as you could wish to meet. He was a bit younger than she was.

Well, she disappeared. Neighbours noticed they'd not seen her about, and when he was asked he gave out she'd gone to visit her auntie. Well, they thought it was funny, for no one had ever heard mention about no auntie. And then it began to come out he'd been seen around. With a girl. One of them young bits of things from his office, all long hair and – well, mini-skirts hadn't hardly come in then, but whatever it was, she wore it. Half his age, keen on music and all that stuff like he was.

People began to come out with they'd been seen about quite a bit long before the wife disappeared – after dark, of course, in the recreation ground down by the pond, or sitting in his car in a side road once or twice. Now they noticed she was going into the house

177

and staying a bit too long. They noticed the car being driven in and out in the night the first weeks, and then, after a month or two, she moved in. Well, that started the tongues wagging even more, and to cut a long story short, the police stepped in.

He didn't deny it. He couldn't, could he, for the girl was living there as bold as brass and too many people had seen them together long before, people at his firm as well as the neighbours. But he said he didn't know nothing about his wife. No, she'd not written. No, she'd not taken her clothes or her Post Office book or the few bits of jewellery her mum had left her, as far as he could tell; only the things she stood up in.

Funny, they said. Had there been any disagreement?

Well, yes he said, there had been a few words. He had to admit it, you see, because the police already knew all about the girl. Had his wife found out about that, they said. No, he said, he'd told her. He wanted to make the break, he said, go away with the girl and marry her, if you please – half his age! Great love, real passion, touching romance, all that sort of nonsense. Disgusting, really. His lawyer made a great thing of it all at the trial but it didn't do any of them much good.

So how had his wife taken it, said the police. Quietly, he said. She'd said she must think it all over and did he know what he was doing? He'd said he did, and she'd said well, one thing was certain and that was she'd never give him his freedom. And he'd said then he'd go off with the girl anyway. And she'd said they must all think it over. There wasn't no row, he said. Next day when he come home from business she'd asked him had he changed his mind and he said he hadn't. She didn't say nothing more, he said, but when he come back from business the next evening she was gone – no note, nothing, just gone.

Well, naturally the police was suspicious. I mean, missing wife, young girl, it's too neat, isn't it? They searched the place, house, garden, recreation ground. And in the pond they found her dentures.

It's not very nice to talk about, but it all come out at the trial and the papers had a field day. Not the full set, just the bottoms, and

178

the dentist checked they were hers. They found a shoe as well and a bangle she used to wear. And buried under the compost heap in the garden they found some underwear.

Well, you can imagine they just tore the place apart after – went through it all with a fine tooth comb, dug up the garden, had dogs and I don't know what – all up and down the path and the grounds, even went out to the sewage farm. But they never found nothing more.

Well, of course they arrested him. They had to. Even without the body it was obvious, wasn't it? They don't like being without the body, of course, but there's several cases they've had to do without, you remember them, I expect. They must have been pretty sure of themselves or they wouldn't have risked proceedings. Of course, it was all circumstantial, but it stood out a mile really. They fair took that sewage farm to pieces, but – well, it's not a very nice subject, is it? No wonder they couldn't find nothing more there, in the circumstances.

It was a big case. His lawyer made a good try for him, I will say that. Made out what a good chap he was, popular, kindly, wouldn't hurt a fly. Tried to make out his wife was a bit of a so-and-so, nagged him about the house and not smoking and wiping his feet, wouldn't have children. Made a great thing about the girl, like I said – great romance, all that stuff, how she'd sold her story to one of the newspapers just so she could pay for his trial, how she'd stand by him for ever, knew he was innocent. The other side soon put paid to that. He hadn't a chance, not with the way the case built up against him – although I will say the jury took their time about reaching the verdict, and one of them said afterwards in a newspaper interview that he was glad they didn't still have them hung.

Well, there it was. He got life. And she got nothing. She never even got him, not even after all her years of waiting, standing by him and all that lark. She'd be down her thirties now – a bit late to start again, especially without him. He'd have been out in a year or so, too, the way they do it now. Life sentence doesn't mean what it used to, more's the pity.

But I think she got the house. It was his, you see, and of course I never claimed it. Well, I couldn't, could I? She's welcome to it, I'm quite content where I am, thank you, with my own little place with no one messing it up and going behind my back and making a fool of me to all the neighbours. Throwing back in my face all the years I gave him, keeping the place nice, keeping respectable – carrying on with a silly bit of a girl young enough to be his daughter, sighing and sobbing, making big speeches, having sex . . . Disgusting.

I had a spare set, you see. It was easy. They was old, didn't fit as well as the ones I dumped in the pond with the other things after dark, but I found a good dentist up north after a year or two when the case was all forgotten, and he soon fixed me up. I took just the housekeeping and a coat I never wore much and pawned my engagement ring and got on the train with no one any the wiser. I touched up my hair a bit next day and wore my glasses and no one ever gave me a second look. They mind their own business up north. It was days before anyone knew I was gone except Frank, and he was keeping quiet about it naturally.

I never meant to come back really. Let them fry, I thought. But I'll go down to the house tomorrow, see if she's still there. Loss of memory, I'll say. No one can prove different.

I can't wait to see her face.

*

Old Tom

*

The trees stand close together at the top of a hill. The hill slopes down to crisscrossing tarmac paths, then down again and on to the limits of the common. The trees cluster, bare-trunked up from the bare earth; nothing will grow beneath them. Branches too almost bare now, for it is the beginning of autumn.

The trees stand black in the darkness; there is no sound. Birds sleep, small creatures do not come here but live and forage in the gorse and scrub of more sheltered areas. Beneath and beyond the hill and the grass the pinkish glow of the city seems to draw all life from the empty slopes. There are only the trees, bare in the darkness, standing close to each other, rough-barked, old, weathered.

One of them is a man. He stands close among the closest trees, still as a tree, tall and straight as their trunks. He must stand so, shielded by them, or Dad will catch him. He wears an old Army greatcoat, its buttons long gone, tied about the waist with string. The glow from down there is from the kitchen; he's safe behind the cupboard door if he don't move. Under the greatcoat is an old jacket, a ravelled pullover, a shirt grey once, and now; under that, leather-brown skin, encrusted dirt that stirs in the creases. If he don't move Dad'll think he's safe asleep. Over his shoulder hangs a battered airline bag, its zipper broken; PANAM, its says. At his feet lolls a supermarket's plastic bag; it is stuffed with newspapers, bits of food, old socks, his Army paybook, a cutting showing King George VI taking the salute soon after VE-day. Treasures. Dad mustn't find them.

There are no socks inside the stained plimsolls but he does not feel the earth's cold seeping through. He must not stir. Beneath a hat, wetted and battered out of shape, merged with the hair that straggles beneath it, Old Tom's gaunt face is alert. Dirt lies in its wrinkles and the stubble of his chin, but the bones are bold still. He has most of his teeth. His eyes, in their deep sockets, are sharp. When Dad slams the back door it will be safe to move. Not till.

In the morning the woman prunes ramblers. It is early yet, she knows, but they have got so overgrown now that her husband is no longer here to deal with them. He loved pruning roses. Nothing else, certainly not the lawn. She could manage that, but the roses . . . ? Ruthless, she knows; cut right down and they will come again. But, knowing death now, she cannot bring herself to kill. Death's sting is here all right – in the worm, the slug, the aphid, the straggling sucker; the empty rooms. Room. Her room now.

Cut, snip, be ruthless. Life will come again in the roses. Not in the house.

There is a movement by the wall. She turns her head. An old black cat has jumped down on to the flowerbed and stands frozen at the sight of her. His fur is shabby, one ear is flat and ragged; his eyes in his wide black mask are limegreen and stark with shock.

They stare at one another. She should clap her hands at him, for cats dig holes in gardens. He stares, unblinking. 'Well, cat?' she says quietly.

Still staring, his shock abates. Tension but not wariness leaves his boney frame. Averting his green gaze, he begins to move, one paw at a time, away through the michaelmas daisies. His tail twitches – she can see now that its tip is not quite straight, broken at some time. Paw by slow paw he turns away, aware of every possibility of terror, rigid with dignity. He is lame in his hindleg but it moves easily, long forgotten. He reaches the fence and, suddenly swift, squeezes through out of sight.

The woman smiles. Sighs. Life. She abandons the roses and goes inside.

When the weather is fine Old Tom stays close to the common. He knows the dells and spinneys, the hollows under the viaduct by the pond, the wooden shelters by the Sports ground, the many litter-bins in which a variety of food scraps can be found, old shoes sometimes, even torn clothing. With his two bundles beside him he sits for hours on a seat on the hillside below the night-time wood, above the spread city. No one disturbs him. People sit on another seat, for he looks forbidding and he smells. Sometimes a gang of boys will jeer at him. 'What's in the bag, Dad? Won the pools, Dad?' He looks at them with his innocent eyes. 'Where's your Ma, Tom? Your Ma's a whore, Tom. Your Dad in the nick, Tom?' His eyes grow wild and he tries to rise, mumbling and waving his ragged arms. Afraid, the boys run off. 'Go piss yourself, Dad!' they shout over the grass. He shuffles his bags together, trembling, and moves away down the hill. He will be strapped for pissing himself, the orphanage master will take no excuses.

Down the hill, where the roads are, he makes for the bus terminus. There is a shelter there and the bus crews pay no attention to him if he sits there hour after hour. Sometimes he even stretches out on the bench, his bundles a pillow, and sleeps; but passengers object, especially if it is raining. 'Come on, Dad, on your way.' Kindly or angrily, the inspectors know him. 'You can't doss here, Dad. Get off to the Haven.'

The Haven is down the street, a battered three-storey terrace house with bare floors and shabby, scarred furniture. Young men and a few women cook for and listen to the men and some women who drift in from the pavements. There is hot soup and pies; tea can be brewed in the bleak kitchen; wine and meths are surreptitiously slurped in the lavatories or the backyard or the dormitories after dark and instantly confiscated if discovered. No one is turned away; you can get a bed there for nothing.

Old Tom has tried it. It is not for him, even in the rain. They're all thieves there. Sleep with your treasures under your head, they're still thieves. Vera's ring, and her picture, where'd they go, eh? Never sold it, though it was 9-carat, hung on a string round

183

his neck. Gone. Years ago when he first started wandering. Found his way about, roads, settlements, handouts. Soup kitchens, coffee stalls, wild men and women on bomb sites, bonfires. Thieves. Where'd her picture go, then? In a little gold frame. Safe in his battledress pocket all those years and then gone from his bags at one of them Havens. She'd not like it. 'You're a softie, Tom. You need to look out for yourself. Stick up for yourself, Tom. I'll stand by you, Tom.' Where'd it gone, eh, and her ring? All thieves.

When the weather is fine he goes on past the bus terminus to the bulldozed site where the builders are coming. There are caves and crannies here, old foundations, cellars, passages. Weeds of great beauty have flourished here and make a cover better than houses. And there is food. People, old women mostly, bring and leave food there for the cats which have bred and gone wild here. They bring it in newspapers or cartons or on tin plates. Fresh food, fish all cooked or out of tins, bits of good meat.

Old Tom watches from a wrecked cellar door, merged in the willow-herb. The cats squat watchfully, they know it is time. Their tails twitch, their eyes do not blink. In a sly wave of fur they move out towards the women unloading their food, waiting till they are gone before streaking down to it. Rising and towering, Old Tom scatters all but the fiercest. The old tom holds his ground, hunched over the newspaper, eyes glaring, growling a spiralling yowl.

Old Tom respects him. Each eat.

Through the autumn the woman looks out of her windows and often sees the old cat limping across her grass. He goes un-hurriedly, with an eye to the house but no fear. Sometimes he pauses and through the glass they regard each other. She makes no movement and after a moment he goes on, dot-and-carry, the fur over his thin ribs dull, his ear squashed, his tail bent at the tip.

It is a warm November, the french window is open. For some days she has put a saucer of milk where it might catch his eye but she has not seen him. Now, sitting inside, trying to answer the letters that still come to her praising her husband, she sees the old cat crossing the grass.

She stills. He pauses. His eyes search, his blunt nose sniffs. Sniffs. It is near, luxury. Slowly, close to the ground, ears flat, he approaches. Sniffs. Looks about, green eyes hard. Hunches, begins to lap. Pink tongue in and out like the tick of a clock. Pause, take care, make sure. All well, hunch, lap. Lick the saucer clean. And again. Rise. Lick lips, twitch tail, give a last look up through the glass where the woman watches. Turn and limp leisurely away.

The woman smiles.

December is wet, January cold. The old women do not come so often to the building site, and the cats are less easy to disperse. People do not walk so often on the hills of the common and the litter-bins contain little but paper and plastic. There is soup and a pie at the Haven but more people too. They crowd him. Get your fucking arse off me legs, Tom, we'll be ashore in a minute, Christ they've got our range, hey Corp, Corp, gives us some room, for fuck's sake, your bleeding pack's in me face, I'll drown in the shallows, I'll sink in me fucking boots, I'll die in the sand, in the dunes, in the scrub ... Where's Vera's ring, eh? Where's her photo? Thieves, all thieves.

In the cold dusk he prowls. Silent in his dirty plimsolls, grey as the twilight, he explores dustbins and garbage sacks. In the back entries to restaurants there are often treasures – half-eaten chicken joints, hamburgers, bread, cold chips. An apple pie, mouldy; bruised fruit. In cans, dregs of strange fluids. Drinking fountains are turned off now to save freezing, but there are ponds.

Silently, warily, Old Tom raises the dustbin lid. There are peelings and rinds, empty tins. From the side of the house a light shines out on to the path where he stands, he can see a half loaf of bread, harmlessly moulded, and a mutton-bone still with meat on it. Eyes bright at the treasure, he bends his gaunt bundle of body towards it, delicately probing, decently, without greed.

A door opens and the woman steps out.

For an instant they stare at each other, frozen, she a looming shape dark against the bright interior, he a grey ghost, wild and predatory. She catches her breath, he gives a kind of mumbling shout, then turns and blunders away out into the street, dropping the dustbin lid as he goes. She stands, shaken for a moment, her heart thumping. Then steps down and replaces the lid on the dustbin; goes back into the house.

As the weather gets colder the cats on the building site decrease. The weak ones have died or been killed – there are rats, dogs and cars as well as stronger cats. Cold and damp undermine the remainder and influenza creeps in. But the old tom survives. He is not so lean now and his fur has a gloss on it. His tail is as bent, his limp as bad – worse, for the damp affects it; but each day when the woman meets his green gaze through the french window, her heart swells. Slowly she opens the window wide enough for his entry. He steps back, his square black mask with its squashed ear studying her. Then cautiously, he steps in. Just inside is a saucer of milk. Without looking about, he hunches and begins to lap. The woman goes quietly out of the room and when she returns, he is sitting, bent tail wrapped over his forefeet, waiting for what she has brought.

She places it before him. He hunches and eats, rapidly, noisily, flicking his head from side to side. Slowly she reaches out and slowly, slowly strokes her hand over his bony shoulders, his lean ribs, to his stern. He growls but does not cease from eating. At first, weeks ago, she dared not touch him. Even now she dare not touch his head. But this one, slow caress she is now allowed while he chews and licks and swallows down, scours the plate, transfers to finish the milk, and at last, replete, sits up and, with precise, ritual delicacy, begins to wash.

She watches him from her chair. Ears, mask, paws, forelegs;

back legs, claws deftly sieved; tight black balls and pink anus fanatically cleansed; face again, whiskers, ears. Lips licked, green gaze at last serenely meeting hers. A rise, a stretch front and back, a requesting glance. She rises and opens the french window. With a flick of his tail the old tom goes out into the darkness.

'Why not stay with us for a bit, Tom?' asks the young man in charge of the soup and the pies.

Tom just stares.

'It'd be best for your chest, you know, now the winter's come on. Just for the dinners and a bed?'

Tom doesn't answer.

'You could go where you liked in the day, you know that, Tom. You'd be your own master just as you like. Just look on us as your base, like?'

Base was where you were before and where you came back to after. Clanking, rough, sodden, harsh, crush, noise, boots, metal, noise, crush. Basement, with the house in powder and chunks on top of it, stairs still intact but all lies about being safe there. Nothing to see after, the rubble mostly all cleared, just the stairs still showing but empty, the feel of his boots and his pack and the cap on his head as he stood there. 'Sorry, lad. Got compassionate, have you? There's nothing more I can tell you. Tried the Town Hall? A nasty incident, this was. Still, old Adolf knows he's beat now and no mistake.'

Can't stay at the Haven, not under a roof. Only safe under sky. And all thieves. Where's Vera's photo, then? And her ring? Thieves.

There is little cover now on the common. The leaves have all fallen, the bushes are sparse. The shelter by the Sports ground is locked up and the seat in the bus terminus hut has been removed in order that no one shall sleep on it. The building site has been fenced off.

He sits on a bench by the lifts at the Underground station sometimes; the staff leave him alone but the passengers look at him angrily and make him afraid. It is closed soon after midnight. Like a grey, gaunt tree he makes his way silently back to the common, the brim of his rotting hat sagging over his stubbled face, his coat flapping below the waist-tied string, his bags of treasures bulging at his knees. Beneath the hat his eyes peer out, wild and blank and innocent. Behind the door Dad won't see him. He'll be strapped if he pisses the bed. Where's Vera's ring, eh? And her photo?

The old cat finishes. Sits up, washes his face and paws. She fears that his fur has lost some of its gloss, and he is wheezing a bit through his black nose. But he has drunk all his milk, eaten almost all his liver, and under her hand his spine rises slightly in acknowledgement of her caress.

Now, wheezing, he does not go through the whole ritual of the wash but sits for a moment, motionless. Then, lifting his black mask to her, he gives her a long unblinking stare. His eyes are green as jade and within them and their miraculous lenses she believes, with a surge of joy, that she sees love. They stare at each other, timelessly. Then he gets up, stretches, turns his head; she opens the door for him. He steps out, stiffly; and slowly, limpingly, moves off across the snow. His paws leave little holes.

She never sees him again.

VAGRANT FOUND DEAD

The body of Thomas Bradshaw, 76, was found on Northfield Common last Wednesday. Bradshaw, of no fixed address, was a familiar figure in the locality and was affectionately known as Old Tom by householders and social workers. An inquest returned a verdict of Death from natural causes.

FOR THE BEST IN PAPERBACKS, LOOK FOR THE

In every corner of the world, on every subject under the sun, Penguin represents quality and variety – the very best in publishing today.

For complete information about books available from Penguin – including Puffins, Penguin Classics and Arkana – and how to order them, write to us at the appropriate address below. Please note that for copyright reasons the selection of books varies from country to country.

In the United Kingdom: Please write to *Dept E.P., Penguin Books Ltd, Harmondsworth, Middlesex, UB7 0DA.*

If you have any difficulty in obtaining a title, please send your order with the correct money, plus ten per cent for postage and packaging, to *PO Box No 11, West Drayton, Middlesex*

In the United States: Please write to *Dept BA, Penguin, 299 Murray Hill Parkway, East Rutherford, New Jersey 07073*

In Canada: Please write to *Penguin Books Canada Ltd, 2801 John Street, Markham, Ontario L3R 1B4*

In Australia: Please write to the *Marketing Department, Penguin Books Australia Ltd, P.O. Box 257, Ringwood, Victoria 3134*

In New Zealand: Please write to the *Marketing Department, Penguin Books (NZ) Ltd, Private Bag, Takapuna, Auckland 9*

In India: Please write to *Penguin Overseas Ltd, 706 Eros Apartments, 56 Nehru Place, New Delhi, 110019*

In the Netherlands: Please write to *Penguin Books Netherlands B.V., Postbus 195, NL–1380AD Weesp*

In West Germany: Please write to *Penguin Books Ltd, Friedrichstrasse 10–12, D–6000 Frankfurt/Main 1*

In Spain: Please write to *Longman Penguin España, Calle San Nicolas 15, E–28013 Madrid*

In Italy: Please write to *Penguin Italia s.r.l., Via Como 4, I-20096 Pioltello (Milano)*

In France: Please write to *Penguin Books Ltd, 39 Rue de Montmorency, F-75003 Paris*

In Japan: Please write to *Longman Penguin Japan Co Ltd, Yamaguchi Building, 2–12–9 Kanda Jimbocho, Chiyoda-Ku, Tokyo 101*

FOR THE BEST IN PAPERBACKS, LOOK FOR THE

CRIME AND MYSTERY IN PENGUINS

Call for the Dead   John Le Carré

The classic work of espionage which introduced the world to George Smiley. 'Brilliant . . . highly intelligent, realistic. Constant suspense. Excellent writing' – *Observer*

Swag   Elmore Leonard

From the bestselling author of *Stick* and *La Brava* comes this wallbanger of a book in which 100,000 dollars' worth of nicely spendable swag sets off a slick, fast-moving chain of events. 'Brilliant' – *The New York Times*

Beast in View   Margaret Millar

'On one level, *Beast in View* is a dazzling conjuring trick. On another it offers a glimpse of bright-eyed madness as disquieting as a shriek in the night. In the whole of Crime Fiction's distinguished sisterhood there is no one quite like Margaret Millar' – *Guardian*

The Julian Symons Omnibus

The Man Who Killed Himself, The Man Whose Dreams Came True, The Man Who Lost His Wife: three novels of cynical humour and cliff-hanging suspense from a master of his craft. 'Exciting and compulsively readable' – *Observer*

Love in Amsterdam   Nicolas Freeling

Inspector Van der Valk's first case involves him in an elaborate cat-and-mouse game with a very wily suspect. 'Has the sinister, spellbinding perfection of a cobra uncoiling. It is a masterpiece of the genre' – Stanley Ellis

Maigret's Pipe   Georges Simenon

Eighteen intriguing cases of mystery and murder to which the pipe-smoking Maigret applies his wit and intuition, his genius for detection and a certain *je ne sais quoi* . . .

CRIME AND MYSTERY IN PENGUINS

Deep Water Patricia Highsmith

Her chilling portrait of a psychopath, from the first faint outline to the full horrors of schizophrenia. 'If you read crime stories at all, or perhaps especially if you don't, you should read *Deep Water*' – Julian Symons in the *Sunday Times*

Farewell, My Lovely Raymond Chandler

Moose Malloy was a big man but not more than six feet five inches tall and not wider than a beer truck. He looked about as inconspicuous as a tarantula on a slice of angel food. Marlowe's greatest case. Chandler's greatest book.

God Save the Child Robert B. Parker

When young Kevin Bartlett disappears, everyone assumes he's run away . . . until the comic strip ransom note arrives . . . 'In classic wisecracking and handfighting tradition, Spenser sorts out the case and wins the love of a fine-boned Jewish Lady . . . who even shares his taste for iced red wine' – Francis Goff in the *Sunday Telegraph*

The Daughter of Time Josephine Tey

Josephine Tey again delves into history to reconstruct a crime. This time it is a crime committed in the tumultuous fifteenth century. 'Most people will find *The Daughter of Time* as interesting and enjoyable a book as they will meet in a month of Sundays' – Marghanita Laski in the *Observer*

The Michael Innes Omnibus

Three tensely exhilarating novels. 'A master – he constructs a plot that twists and turns like an electric eel: it gives you shock upon shock and you cannot let go' – *The Times Literary Supplement*

Killer's Choice Ed McBain

Who killed Annie Boone? Employer, lover, ex-husband, girlfriend? This is a tense, terrifying and tautly written novel from the author of *The Mugger*, *The Pusher*, *Lady Killer* and a dozen other first class thrillers.